Buck

HENRY HUGGINS

HENRY

BY BEVERLY CLEARY

HUGGINS

ILLUSTRATED BY
LOUIS DARLING

A YEARLING BOOK

Published by
Dell Publishing
a division of
The Bantam Doubleday Dell Publishing Group, Inc.
666 Fifth Avenue
New York. New York 10103

ISBN: 0-440-43551-X

Reprinted by arrangement with William Morrow & Company, New York
Printed in the United States of America

May 1979

30 29 28 27 26 25 24

CW

CONTENTS

Chapter

CHAPTER ONE

Henry
and Ribs

HENRY HUGGINS was in the third grade. His hair looked like a scrubbing brush and most of his grown-up front teeth were in. He lived with his mother and father in a square white house on Klickitat Street. Except for having his tonsils out when he was six and breaking his arm falling out of a cherry tree when he was seven, nothing much happened to Henry.

I wish something exciting would happen, Henry often thought.

But nothing very interesting ever happened to Henry, at least not until one Wednesday after-noon in March. Every Wednesday after school

Henry rode downtown on the bus to go swimming at the Y.M.C.A. After he swam for an hour, he got on the bus again and rode home just in time for dinner. It was fun but not really exciting.

When Henry left the Y.M.C.A. on this particular Wednesday, he stopped to watch a man tear down a circus poster. Then, with three nickels and one dime in his pocket, he went to the corner drugstore to buy a chocolate ice cream cone. He thought he would eat the ice cream cone, get on the bus, drop his dime in the slot, and ride home.

That is not what happened.

He bought the ice cream cone and paid for it with one of his nickels. On his way out of the drugstore he stopped to look at funny books. It was a free look, because he had only two nickels left.

He stood there licking his chocolate ice cream cone and reading one of the funny books when he heard a thump, thump, thump. Henry turned, and there behind him was a dog. The dog was scratching himself. He wasn't any special kind of dog. He was too small to be a big dog but, on the other hand, he was much too big to be a little dog. He wasn't a white dog, because parts of him were brown and other parts were black and in between there were yellowish patches. His ears stood up and his tail was long and thin.

The dog was hungry. When Henry licked, he licked. When Henry swallowed, he swallowed.

"Hello, you old dog," Henry said. "You can't have my ice cream cone."

Swish, swish, swish went the tail. "Just one bite," the dog's brown eyes seemed to say.

"Go away," ordered Henry. He wasn't very firm about it. He patted the dog's head.

The tail wagged harder. Henry took one last lick. "Oh, all right," he said. "If you're that hungry, you might as well have it."

The ice cream cone disappeared in one gulp.

"Now go away," Henry told the dog. "I have to catch a bus for home."

He started for the door. The dog started, too.

"Go away, you skinny old dog." Henry didn't say it very loudly. "Go on home."

The dog sat down at Henry's feet. Henry looked at the dog and the dog looked at Henry.

"I don't think you've got a home. You're awful thin. Your ribs show right through your skin."

Thump, thump, thump replied the tail.

"And you haven't got a collar," said Henry.

He began to think. If only he could keep the dog! He had always wanted a dog of his very own and now he had found a dog that wanted him. He couldn't go home and leave a hungry dog on the street corner. If only he knew what his mother and father would say! He fingered the two nickels in his pocket. That was it! He would use one of the nickels to phone his mother.

"Come on, Ribsy. Come on, Ribs, old boy. I'm going to call you Ribsy because you're so thin."

The dog trotted after the boy to the telephone booth in the corner of the drugstore. Henry shoved him into the booth and shut the door. He had never used a pay telephone before. He had to put the telephone book on the floor and stand on tiptoe on it to reach the mouthpiece. He gave the operator his number and dropped his nickel into the coin box.

"Hello—Mom?"

"Why, Henry!" His mother sounded surprised. "Where are you?"

"At the drugstore near the Y."

Ribs began to scratch. Thump, thump, thump. Inside the telephone booth the thumps sounded loud and hollow.

"For goodness' sake, Henry, what's that noise?" his mother demanded. Ribs began to whimper and then to howl. "Henry," Mrs. Huggins shouted, "are you all right?"

"Yes, I'm all right," Henry shouted back. He never could understand why his mother always thought something had happened to him when nothing ever did. "That's just Ribsy."

"Ribsy?" His mother was exasperated. "Henry, will you please tell me what is going on?"

"I'm trying to," said Henry. Ribsy howled louder. People were gathering around the phone booth to see what was going on. "Mother, I've found a dog. I sure wish I could keep him. He's a good dog and I'd feed him and wash him and everything. Please, Mom."

"I don't know, dear," his mother said. "You'll have to ask your father."

"Mom!" Henry wailed. "That's what you always say!" Henry was tired of standing on tiptoe and the phone booth was getting warm. "Mom, please say yes and I'll never ask for another thing as long as I live!"

"Well, all right, Henry. I guess there isn't any reason why you shouldn't have a dog. But you'll have to bring him home on the bus. Your father has the car today and I can't come after you. Can you manage?"

"Sure! Easy."

"And Henry, please don't be late. It looks as if it might rain."

"All right, Mom." Thump, thump, thump.

"Henry, what's that thumping noise?"

"It's my dog, Ribsy. He's scratching a flea."

"Oh, Henry," Mrs. Huggins moaned. "Couldn't you have found a dog without fleas?"

Henry thought that was a good time to hang up. "Come on, Ribs," he said. "We're going home on the bus."

When the big green bus stopped in front of the drugstore, Henry picked up his dog. Ribsy was heavier than he expected. He had a hard time getting him into the bus and was wondering how he would get a dime out of his pocket when the driver said, "Say, sonny, you can't take that dog on the bus."

"Why not?" asked Henry.

"It's a company rule, sonny. No dogs on buses."

"Golly, Mister, how'm I going to get him home? I just have to get him home."

"Sorry, sonny. I didn't make the rule. No animal can ride on a bus unless it's inside a box."

"Well, thanks anyway," said Henry doubtfully, and lifted Ribsy off the bus.

"Well, I guess we'll have to get a box. I'll get you onto the next bus somehow," promised Henry.

He went back into the drugstore followed closely by Ribsy. "Have you got a big box I could have, please?" he asked the man at the toothpaste counter. "I need one big enough for my dog."

The clerk leaned over the counter to look at Ribsy. "A cardboard box?" he asked.

"Yes, please," said Henry, wishing the man would hurry. He didn't want to be late getting home.

The clerk pulled a box out from under the counter. "This hair tonic carton is the only one I have. I guess it's big enough, but why anyone would want to put a dog in a cardboard box I can't understand."

The box was about two feet square and six

inches deep. On one end was printed, "Don't Let Them Call You Baldy," and on the other, "Try Our Large Economy Size."

Henry thanked the clerk, carried the box out to the bus stop, and put it on the sidewalk. Ribsy padded after him. "Get in, fellow," Henry commanded. Ribsy understood. He stepped into the box and sat down just as the bus came around the corner. Henry had to kneel to pick up the box. It was not a very strong box and he had to put his arms under it. He staggered as he lifted it, feeling like the strong man who lifted weights at the circus. Ribsy lovingly licked his face with his wet pink tongue.

"Hey, cut that out!" Henry ordered. "You better be good if you're going to ride on the bus with me."

The bus stopped at the curb. When it was Henry's turn to get on, he had trouble finding the step because he couldn't see his feet. He had to try several times before he hit it. Then he discovered he had forgotten to take his dime out of his pocket. He was afraid to put the box down for fear Ribsy might escape.

He turned sideways to the driver and asked politely, "Will you please take the dime out of my pocket for me? My hands are full."

The driver pushed his cap back on his head and exclaimed, "Full! I should say they *are* full! And just where do you think you're going with that animal?"

"Home," said Henry in a small voice.

The passengers were staring and most of them were smiling. The box was getting heavier every minute.

"Not on this bus, you're not!" said the driver.

"But the man on the last bus said I could take the dog on the bus in a box," protested Henry, who was afraid he couldn't hold the dog much longer. "He said it was a company rule."

"He meant a big box tied shut. A box with holes punched in it for the dog to breathe through."

Henry was horrified to hear Ribsy growl. "Shut up," he ordered.

Ribsy began to scratch his left ear with his left hind foot. The box began to tear. Ribsy jumped out of the box and off the bus and Henry jumped after him. The bus pulled away with a puff of exhaust.

"Now see what you've done! You've spoiled everything." The dog hung his head and tucked his tail between his legs. "If I can't get you home, how can I keep you?"

Henry sat down on the curb to think. It was so late and the clouds were so dark that he didn't want to waste time looking for a big box. His mother was probably beginning to worry about him.

People were stopping on the corner to wait for the next bus. Among them Henry noticed an elderly lady carrying a large paper shopping bag full of apples. The shopping bag gave him an idea. Jumping up, he snapped his fingers at Ribs and ran back into the drugstore.

"You back again?" asked the toothpaste clerk. "What do you want this time? String and paper to wrap your dog in?"

"No, sir," said Henry. "I want one of those big nickel shopping bags." He laid his last nickel on the counter.

"Well, I'll be darned," said the clerk, and handed the bag across the counter.

Henry opened the bag and set it up on the floor. He picked up Ribsy and shoved him hind feet first into the bag. Then he pushed his front feet in. A lot of Ribsy was left over.

The clerk was leaning over the counter watching. "I guess I'll have to have some string and paper, too," Henry said, "if I can have some free."

"Well! Now I've seen everything." The clerk shook his head as he handed a piece of string and a big sheet of paper across the counter.

Ribsy whimpered, but he held still while Henry wrapped the paper loosely around his head and shoulders and tied it with the string. The dog made a lumpy package, but by taking one handle of the bag in each hand Henry was able to carry it to the bus stop. He didn't think the bus driver would notice him. It was getting dark and a crowd of people, most of them with packages, was waiting on the corner. A few spatters of rain hit the pavement.

This time Henry remembered his dime. Both hands were full, so he held the dime in his teeth and stood behind the woman with the bag of apples. Ribsy wiggled and whined, even though Henry tried to pet him through the paper. When the bus stopped, he climbed on behind the lady, quickly set the bag down, dropped his dime in the slot, picked up the bag, and squirmed through the crowd to a seat beside a fat man near the back of the bus.

"Whew!" Henry sighed with relief. The driver was the same one he had met on the first bus! But Ribs was on the bus at last. Now if he could only keep him quiet for fifteen minutes they would be home and Ribsy would be his for keeps.

The next time the bus stopped Henry saw Scooter McCarthy, a fifth grader at school, get on and make his way through the crowd to the back of the bus.

Just my luck, thought Henry. I'll bet he wants to know what's in my bag.

"Hi," said Scooter.

"Hi," said Henry.

"Whatcha got in that bag?" asked Scooter.

"None of your beeswax," answered Henry.

Scooter looked at Henry. Henry looked at Scooter. Crackle, crackle, crackle went the bag. Henry tried to hold it more tightly between his knees.

"There's something alive in that bag!" Scooter said accusingly.

"Shut up, Scooter!" whispered Henry.

"Aw, shut up yourself!" said Scooter. "You've got something alive in that bag!"

By this time the passengers at the back of the bus were staring at Henry and his package. Crackle, crackle, crackle. Henry tried to pat Ribsy again through the paper. The bag crackled even louder. Then it began to wiggle.

"Come on, tell us what's in the bag," coaxed the fat man.

"N-n-n-nothing," stammered Henry. "Just something I found."

"Maybe it's a rabbit," suggested one passenger. "I think it's kicking."

"No, it's too big for a rabbit," said another.

"I'll bet it's a baby," said Scooter. "I'll bet you kidnaped a baby!"

"I did not!"

Ribs began to whimper and then to howl. Crackle, crackle, crackle. Thump, thump, thump. Ribsy scratched his way out of the bag.

"Well, I'll be doggoned!" exclaimed the fat man and began to laugh. "I'll be doggoned!"

"It's just a skinny old dog," said Scooter.

"He is not! He's a good dog."

Henry tried to keep Ribsy between his knees. The bus lurched around a corner and started to go uphill. Henry was thrown against the fat man. The frightened dog wiggled away from him, squirmed between the passengers, and started for the front of the bus.

"Here, Ribsy, old boy! Come back here," called Henry and started after him.

"E-e-ek! A dog!" squealed the lady with the bag of apples. "Go away, doggie, go away!"

Ribsy was scared. He tried to run and crashed into the lady's bag of apples. The bag tipped over and the apples began to roll toward the back of the bus, which was grinding up a steep hill. The apples rolled around the feet of the people who were standing. Passengers began to slip and slide. They dropped their packages and grabbed one another.

Crash! A high-school girl dropped an armload of books.

Rattle! Bang! Crash! A lady dropped a big paper bag. The bag broke open and pots and pans rolled out.

Thud! A man dropped a coil of garden hose. The hose unrolled and the passengers found it wound around their legs.

People were sitting on the floor. They were sitting on books and apples. They were even sitting on other people's laps. Some of them had their hats over their faces and their feet in the air.

Skree-e-etch! The driver threw on the brakes

and turned around in his seat just as Henry made his way through the apples and books and pans and hose to catch Ribsy.

The driver pushed his cap back on his head. "O.K., sonny," he said to Henry. "Now you know why dogs aren't allowed on buses!"

"Yes, sir," said Henry in a small voice. "I'm sorry."

"You're sorry! A lot of good that does. Look at this bus! Look at those people!"

"I didn't mean to make any trouble," said Henry. "My mother said I could keep the dog if I could bring him home on the bus."

The fat man began to snicker. Then he chuckled. Then he laughed and then he roared. He laughed until tears streamed down his cheeks and all the other passengers were laughing too, even the man with the hose and the lady with the apples.

The driver didn't laugh. "Take that dog and get off the bus!" he ordered. Ribsy whimpered and tucked his tail between his legs.

The fat man stopped laughing. "See here, driver," he said, "you can't put that boy and his dog off in the rain."

"Well, he can't stay on the bus," snapped the driver.

Henry didn't know what he was going to do. He guessed he'd have to walk the rest of the way home. He wasn't sure he knew the way in the dark.

Just then a siren screamed. It grew louder and louder until it stopped right alongside the bus.

A policeman appeared in the entrance. "Is there a boy called Henry Huggins on this bus?" he asked.

"Oh boy, you're going to be arrested for having a dog on the bus!" gloated Scooter. "I'll bet you have to go to jail!"

"I'm him," said Henry in a very small voice.

"I am he," corrected the lady with the apples, who had been a schoolteacher and couldn't help correcting boys.

"You'd better come along with us," said the policeman.

"Boy, you're sure going to get it!" said Scooter.

"Surely going to get it," corrected the apple lady.

Henry and Ribsy followed the policeman off the bus and into the squad car, where Henry and the dog sat in the back seat.

"Are you going to arrest me?" Henry asked timidly.

"Well, I don't know. Do you think you ought to be arrested?"

"No, sir," said Henry politely. He thought the policeman was joking, but he wasn't sure. It was

hard to tell about grownups sometimes. "I didn't mean to do anything. I just had to get Ribsy home. My mother said I could keep him if I could bring him home on the bus."

"What do you think?" the officer asked his partner, who was driving the squad car.

"We-e-ell, I think we might let him off this time," answered the driver. "His mother must be pretty worried about him if she called the police, and I don't think she'd want him to go to jail."

"Yes, he's late for his dinner already. Let's see how fast we can get him home."

The driver pushed a button and the siren began to shriek. Ribsy raised his head and howled. The tires sucked at the wet pavement and the windshield wipers splip-splopped. Henry began to enjoy himself. Wouldn't this be something to tell the kids at school! Automobiles pulled over to the curb as the police car went faster and faster. Even the bus Henry had been on had to pull over and stop. Henry waved to the passengers. They waved back. Up the hill the police car sped and around the corner until they came to Klickitat Street and then to Henry's block and then pulled up in front of his house.

Henry's mother and father were standing on the porch waiting for him. The neighbors were looking out of their windows.

"Well!" said his father after the policeman had gone. "It's about time you came home. So this is Ribsy! I've heard about you, fellow, and there's a big bone and a can of Feeley's Flea Flakes waiting for you."

"Henry, what *will* you do next?" sighed his mother.

"Golly, Mom, I didn't do anything. I just brought my dog home on the bus like you said."

Ribsy sat down and began to scratch.

CHAPTER TWO

Gallons
of Guppies

EVERY afternoon after school Ribsy waited for Henry under a fir tree in the corner of the school yard. Four days a week they ran home the shortest way, past the park, up the hill, and through the vacant lot.

On Fridays, however, they walked home the long way round past the Rose City Drugstore, the Supermarket, the Ideal Barber Shop, and the Lucky Dog Pet Shop. At the pet store they stopped while Henry bought two pounds of horse meat from Mr. Pennycuff.

Henry liked to go to the pet store. The windows were full of puppies and kittens and, just before

Easter, rabbits and baby chicks and ducks. Inside there was usually a parrot or monkey and once there had been a deodorized skunk. Henry thought it would be fun to have a skunk following him around, but when he found it cost forty dollars he gave up the idea.

But best of all Henry liked the fish. One side of the store was covered with rows of little tanks. Each aquarium contained green plants that grew under water, snails, and a different kind of tropi-

cal fish. Henry always stopped to look into each tank. He liked the dollar-sized black-and-silver-striped angelfish and the inch-long orange moon-fish with their velvety fins and tails. He thought the tiny catfish were fun to watch, because they stayed on the bottom of the tanks, rolled their eyes, and used their whisker-like barbels to feel around in the sand for food. Mr. Pennycuff explained that the fish came from all over the world, but most of them came from jungle rivers where the water was warm. That was why they were called tropical fish.

One Friday when Henry went to the pet store he saw a sign that read:

SPECIAL OFFER

1 pair of guppies
fish bowl
1 snail
aquatic plant
package of fish food

ALL FOR 79¢

"Jeepers!" said Henry. "All that for seventy-nine cents!" He looked at the fish in the bowls. Each bowl held one plain silvery-gray fish almost two inches long and one smaller fish with all the colors of the rainbow. "That really is a bargain!"

"It certainly is," agreed Mr. Pennycuff. "Shall I wrap up a pair for you?"

Henry felt around in his pocket. The silver dollar his grandfather had given him was still there. He watched the little rainbow fish chase the silvery fish and decided he had to have a pair of guppies. After all, it was his very own money he was spending. He would keep them on the dresser in his room. They would just stay in his room and swim quietly around in their bowl. He didn't see how his mother could object to two quiet little fish that didn't bark or track in mud or anything.

"I'll take a pair," Henry told Mr. Pennycuff, and watched him fasten waxed paper around the top of the bowl with a rubber band and put it into a bag.

"Now be sure to put the bowl near a heater in cold weather so the fish won't get chilled and catch ick."

"Ick?" said Henry.

"Yes, ick. It's short for *ichthyophthirius*. When the fish get chilled, they catch ick and are covered with tiny white spots."

"Gosh," said Henry. Maybe there was more to keeping guppies than he thought.

"Oh, don't worry," said Mr. Pennycuff. "They can stand water down to sixty degrees. If it were that cold in the house, you'd have the heat on."

That sounded easy. "How often do I change the water?" asked Henry.

"You shouldn't have to change the water. The snails help keep it clean. Just give the fish a tiny pinch of food once a day. It's only when the fish don't eat all their food or when you have too many fish in a bowl that the water gets dirty." Mr. Pennycuff gave Henry his change.

"I didn't know that," said Henry. "I'm glad you

told me. Here, Ribsy." He handed Ribsy his package of horse meat. The dog took it in his mouth and they left the pet store. "You'll have to carry your meat all the way home today. And don't you stop and try to eat it before we get home, either. It has to last you a few days."

Ribs wagged his tail and trotted on ahead of Henry with his meat. Henry tried to walk without jiggling the package. He didn't want to slosh the guppies any more than he had to. When Ribsy was half a block ahead of Henry, he dropped his package and looked back at Henry. Then he began to tear the paper off the meat.

"Hey! Cut that out!" yelled Henry. He started to run but the water in his fish bowl sloshed and he had to stop.

Just to be safe Ribsy picked up his meat, trotted farther down the sidewalk, and finished tearing off the paper.

"Stop that! You—you—you old dog!" Again Henry tried to run. This time he held the bowl straight out in front of him, but the water still sloshed.

Ribs gobbled part of the meat and then trotted ahead with the rest of it in his mouth. Just as Henry was almost close enough to reach for the meat, Ribsy put on a burst of speed.

"Ribsy! You come here!" The dog ignored Henry. "I'll get you for this!" Henry was really angry now. He set his package of guppies on the sidewalk and ran after his dog. This time Henry caught up with him.

Henry grabbed one end of the meat and pulled. Ribsy, growling deep in his throat, hung onto the other end and pulled. The dog had a better grip on the meat because he could sink his teeth into it. Henry found that raw meat was cold and slippery.

"You let go that meat!"

Ribsy growled more fiercely. He sounded as if he meant it. The harder Henry pulled, the louder Ribsy growled.

Henry was sure Ribsy wouldn't really bite him, but just the same he knew it was not a good idea to  annoy any animal when it was eating. Anyway, he couldn't stand there all afternoon playing tug-of-war with a piece of horse meat. His guppies might get cold.

"All right, you old dog! Go ahead and eat it and see if I care. You'll just have to eat canned dog food the rest of the week." He went back to his guppies while Ribsy wolfed the rest of the meat, licked his chops, and then, with his stomach bulging, followed slowly at Henry's heels the rest of the way home.

When they reached Henry's house on Klickitat Street, Henry opened the door and yelled, "Hey, Mom! Come and see what I bought with the silver dollar Grandpa gave me."

"I'm afraid to look," answered his mother from the kitchen. "What is it this time?"

"Fish."

"Fish?" Mrs. Huggins sounded surprised. "Did you want me to cook it for dinner?"

Henry carried his package into the kitchen. "No, Mom, you don't understand. Not dead fish. Live fish swimming around in a bowl of water. They're called guppies."

"Guppies?"

"Yes. Just two little fish. I'll keep them on my dresser and they won't be any trouble at all. They were on sale at the pet shop. They were a bargain. See, Mom?" Henry gently lifted the fish bowl out of the bag.

Mrs. Huggins put down the potato she was peeling. "Why, Henry, what pretty little fish!"

"I thought you'd like them." Henry was pleased.

His mother bent closer to the fish bowl. "But, Henry, what are those little dark things in the water?"

"What little dark things?" Henry looked closer.

"Why, they're baby fish," Mrs. Huggins exclaimed. "There must be fifteen or twenty."

"Baby guppies!" Henry was delighted. "Look, Mom, did you ever see such teeny-weeny little fish? Golly, they're so little just about all you can see are their eyes and their tails."

Mrs. Huggins sighed. "Henry, I'm afraid they won't be teeny-weeny little fish very long. They'll grow and then what are you going to do with them?"

"I don't know. I'll ask Dad." Henry was worried. "Maybe he knows about baby guppies."

But when Mr. Huggins came home from work, Henry was disappointed to learn that he knew nothing about little guppies. "Why don't you get a book about guppies from the library?" he suggested.

Mrs. Huggins said there would be time before dinner, so Henry found his library card and he and Ribsy ran all the way to the library.

"Hello, Henry," said the lady in the boys and girls' room at the library. "Have you come for another book about gienats and orges?"

This was a joke between the librarian and Henry. When Henry had first started reading fairy tales by himself he returned a book and asked for another about gienats and orges. He felt a little silly about it now, although he secretly thought gienats and orges sounded better than giants and ogres.

"No, I want a book about guppies," Henry answered. "I have some baby guppies and I don't know how to take care of them."

The librarian found a book on hobbies with a chapter on fish, but it did not tell much about guppies. "Just a minute, Henry," she said. "Maybe there is something in the adult room." She returned with a thick book about tropical fish. It was full of colored pictures. "I'm sure this will help you," she said, "but I'm afraid it's too hard for you to read. I'll let you take it out on your card if you think your mother and father will help you with it."

"Sure, my dad will help me."

The librarian stamped the book on his card and Henry, proud to have a grown-up book stamped on his library card, ran home with it.

After dinner Mr. Huggins sat down to read the fish book while Henry went to his room to watch his guppies. This time he counted thirty-eight babies. After a while his father came in with the book in his hand. "This is a mighty interesting book, Henry, but you're going to need some more fish bowls. According to this book you can't keep so many fish in one bowl."

"But, Dad, where will I get more bowls?"

"Maybe we can find something in the basement."

So Henry and his father rummaged through the basement until they found a gallon jar Mrs. Huggins used for making dill pickles.

"This should do," said Mr. Huggins. They carried it upstairs and washed it. Mr. Huggins filled it with hot water and carried it into Henry's room. "Now when the water cools we can move some of the little guppies. They can't live in cold water right out of the faucet. They need water that has stood or hot water that has cooled. While it's cooling, we can make a net." He found a piece of wire and bent it into a circle. Mrs. Huggins took an old stocking and sewed it to the wire to make a little fish net.

Henry and his father took turns catching the tiny fish with the net and moving them into the pickle jar. Henry was surprised that such small fish could swim so fast.

The next day and every day after that Henry looked at his guppies the first thing in the morning. When he came home from school he looked at his guppies before he went into the kitchen for something to eat. His fish grew and grew. As the weeks passed the big guppies had more little guppies. The little guppies grew up to be big guppies and had little guppies of their own. Henry had hundreds of guppies. He couldn't find any more pickle jars so he started using his mother's quart fruit jars. He couldn't keep many fish in a quart of water.

Henry had jars on his dresser. He had them on the table by his bed. He put jars on the floor all around the edge of his room. When he had one row of jars all the way around the floor, he started another row.

"Goodness, Henry," his mother said, "pretty soon you won't be able to walk in here."

"If you keep all your guppies," said his father, "by the end of the year you'll have over a million fish in your bedroom!"

"Golly!" said Henry. "A million fish in my bedroom!" Wouldn't that be something to tell the kids at school!

Henry was glad when summer vacation started. It took him so long to feed his fish that he no longer had time to play with the other children on

Klickitat Street. He spent all his allowance on fish food, snails, and plants for his jars. He slept with his windows shut if he thought the night were going to be cold. He wasn't going to have his fish getting sick if he could help it.

All day long the boys and girls in the neighborhood rang the doorbell and asked to see Henry's fish.

Finally his mother said, "Henry, this can't go on. You must get rid of some of those fish. You'll have to give them to your friends."

Henry liked each fish so much he couldn't decide which one he liked best. They were all so

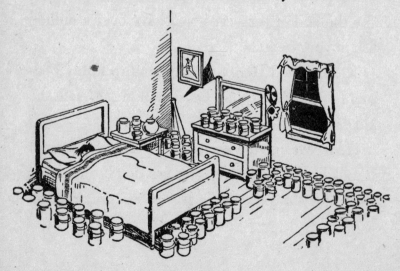

lively, swimming around in their fruit jars. Henry didn't see how he could part with any of them, but now that he was on the third row of jars around his room, he decided to try. He started asking his friends in the neighborhood if they would like to have some fish.

Scooter didn't think he had time to take care of fish. He delivered the *Shopping News* two days a week.

Mary Jane said her mother wouldn't let her have any fish. Mary Jane's mother was very particular.

Robert said he would rather come over and look at Henry's fish than take care of guppies of his own.

Finally Beezus said she would take one fish. Beezus' real name was Beatrice, but her little sister Ramona called her Beezus and now everyone else did too. Beezus and Ramona already had a cat, three white rats, and a turtle, so one fish wouldn't make much difference. It took Henry a long time to decide which guppy to give her.

Then one morning Mrs. Huggins came home from the Supermarket with three lugs of apricots in the back seat of the car. When Henry helped her carry them into the house, she said, "Henry, run down to the basement and bring up about twenty quart jars. These apricots are so ripe I want to start canning them right away."

Henry went down to the basement. He did not come back with twenty quart jars. He came back with four. "These are all I could find, Mom," he said.

"Oh, dear, and one of them has a crack." Mrs. Huggins looked at the three lugs of apricots. Then she looked at Henry. "Henry," she said, and he knew from the way she said it she meant whatever she was going to say, "go to your room and bring me seventeen quart jars. And don't bring me any jars with guppies in them, either."

"Yes, Mom," said Henry in a meek voice. He went into his room and looked at the jars of guppies. He guessed he did have too many fish. But they were such nice fish! He got down on his hands and knees to look at his pets.

"Henry!" his mother called. "I am starting to pit the apricots. You'll have to hurry!"

"O.K." Henry took his net and started catching the smallest guppies. The only thing he could do was to move them in with the other fish. He hated to do it, because the fish book said they shouldn't be crowded. When the guppies were moved, he carried the jars into the kitchen and poured the water down the sink.

"I'm sorry, Henry," his mother said, "but after all, I did tell you some time ago that you couldn't go on putting guppies in fruit jars."

"I know, Mom. I guess I'll have to think of something else." It took Henry the rest of the morning to feed his fish. He had to put the tiniest pinch of the finest fish food into each jar. He could hear Robert and Beezus playing cowboy in the vacant lot. Ribsy trotted into his room, watched him a few minutes, and then went outdoors. Henry began to wish he were outdoors, too, but he couldn't let his little fish go hungry.

Late that afternoon Mrs. Huggins drove downtown to pick up Henry's father after work. When they returned, Henry saw his father carrying more lugs of apricots into the kitchen. He had a feeling he knew what was coming next.

It came.

"Henry," his mother said, "I am afraid I'll have to ask you for some more fruit jars."

Henry sighed. "I guess I'll have to double them up some more." He started to go to his room and then turned back. "Say, Mom, are you going to can anything besides apricots this year?"

"Yes, tomatoes and pears. And I thought we might go out to Mount Hood and pick huckleberries. You like huckleberry pie during the winter, don't you?"

Henry certainly did like huckleberry pie. He liked it any time of year. He went to his room and moved more of his guppies. Tomatoes, pears, and huckleberries. He could see that his mother would need all her fruit jars before the summer was over. That would leave him his original bowl and the gallon pickle jar.

"Hey, Mom," he yelled. "Are you going to make dill pickles, too?"

"Yes, Henry."

There went the pickle jar. By the end of the summer Henry would have to move the hundreds of fish he had now, and goodness knows how many more, back into the bowl. There would be so many fish there wouldn't be room for any water.

That settled it. Henry decided he would have to get rid of all his guppies. He hated to do it, but if he kept even two he would soon be right back where he was now. It would be nice to have time to play outdoors again. Henry made up his mind to take every one of his fish back to the Lucky Dog Pet Shop. Maybe Mr. Pennycuff could have another sale.

Henry was chasing a guppy with the net when his father came into the room. He told his father what he planned to do. "I sure hate to do it," he mourned, "but I can't keep a million guppies in my bedroom." He looked sorrowfully at his fish.

"I know, Henry. I hate to see the fish go, too, but they're getting out of hand. I'll tell you what to do. Catch all the guppies and put them into the pickle jar. It won't hurt them to be crowded for a little while. Right after supper I'll run you down to the pet shop in the car."

Henry sadly packed up his fish, and after supper he and his father and Ribsy got into the car and drove to the pet shop. Ribsy liked to ride in the car.

"I brought you a lot of guppies," Henry said to Mr. Pennycuff. "I hope you can use them."

"Use them!" exclaimed Mr. Pennycuff. "I certainly can. I haven't had a guppy in this store since the sale. Let's see them."

While Henry unwrapped his pickle jar, his

father looked at the tanks of tropical fish along the wall.

"I should say you do have a lot of guppies," said Mr. Pennycuff. "Nice healthy ones, too. You must have taken good care of them." He held the jar up to the light and looked at it closely. It seethed with gray guppies, rainbow guppies, and baby guppies of all sizes, swimming round and round. "Hmmmm. Let's see. We-e-ell." Mr. Pennycuff continued to stare at the fish.

Henry couldn't understand why he was muttering to himself that way. He had given Mr. Pennycuff the guppies and now he wished he would return the pickle jar so he could go.

"Well, now," said Mr. Pennycuff, "I guess these fish are worth about seven dollars. I can't give it to you in money, but you can pick out seven dollars' worth of anything in the store you want."

Seven dollars! Henry was astounded. Seven dollars' worth of anything in the pet shop! He was rich! He had been so busy thinking about getting rid of the guppies that it had not occurred to him they might be worth something to Mr. Pennycuff.

"Hey, Dad! Did you hear that? Seven dollars!" Henry shouted.

"I certainly did. You'd better start looking around."

"Take anything you want, sonny. Dog collars, kittens, bird seed. Anything."

Henry tried to decide what he would like. Ribsy had a collar and leash and a dish, so he didn't need anything. He looked at the kittens. The sign read, "Kittens. One dollar each." They were cute, but Henry decided he didn't want seven dollars' worth of kittens. Ribsy would chase them.

"You don't have any skunks on sale for seven dollars?" he asked hopefully.

"No, I haven't had any skunks for a long time."

"I'm glad to hear that," said Mr. Huggins.

Henry looked at the tropical fish. Then he looked all around the store and came back to the tropical fish again. He stopped to watch a little catfish busily digging in the sand. Suddenly Henry knew that the only thing in the store he really wanted was more fish.

"Could I keep a catfish in my fish bowl?" he asked Mr. Pennycuff.

"No, sonny, they have to be kept in warm water. They need an electric heater and a thermostat in the water to keep the water the right temperature." He held up two long glass tubes. One looked as if it were filled with sand and the other with wires. "See, this is what I mean. They fit into the corners of an aquarium like this and keep the water warm all the time." He fitted them into the corner of a little tank on a table.

"How much does that cost?"

"The tank is three dollars and the heater and thermostat come to four. That makes seven dollars."

Henry was disappointed. "I wouldn't have any money left for a catfish and the only thing I really want is more fish."

"You know, Henry, I hoped you'd say that," answered his father. "I hated to see those guppies go as much as you did. If you buy the tank and heater and thermostat, I'll buy the fish."

"Gee, Dad, that's swell! Let's get a little cat-fish!" Then Henry thought of something. "Do cat-fish have as many babies as guppies?" he asked Mr. Pennycuff.

"Oh my, no. Catfish rarely have babies when they're kept in tanks. They mostly have them when they live outdoors in ponds and rivers."

"Swell!" said Henry. "That's the kind of fish we want. Won't Mom be surprised!"

CHAPTER THREE

Henry and the
Night Crawlers

WHEN Henry came home from school one Friday late in September, he shook all his nickels and dimes and pennies out of a marble sack onto his bedspread. His expenses had been heavy and he knew he did not have much money left. The first thing he had done after finding Ribsy was to pay for his license and buy him a collar. Naturally he didn't want his dog to eat from an old chipped dish, so he had spent sixty-nine cents for a red plastic dish with D O G printed on it. This nearly exhausted his savings. He had spent his silver dollar on the guppies and all his allowance to take care of them. Then he had sold the guppies for seven dollars and spent all seven for the tank and thermostat for the catfish.

At breakfast this morning his father had given him his weekly twenty-five cents. Besides that, he had six cents saved from last week's allowance. He also had a nickel he had found in the park. And then there was his Canadian dime. He could try to spend that but he hated to after keeping it almost a year. He might want to start a coin collection sometime. With the Canadian dime, he had forty-six cents, not counting nine cents he could get for three old milk bottles he had found in a vacant lot on the way home from school.

It was not enough.

Henry needed thirteen dollars and ninety-five cents plus forty-one cents for tax.

Henry needed all this money because he wanted to buy a football—a real football from a sporting goods store, not just a toy football from a department store. This time he wanted a genuine cowhide football stitched with nylon thread and laced with buckskin thongs. Every boy on Klickitat Street wanted one.

As Henry looked at the money spread out on his bed, he heard someone calling, "He-e-enry!"

Henry went to the front door. There on the front porch stood Scooter McCarthy. Henry was surprised, because Scooter didn't often come to play with him. He was a fifth grader and bigger than Henry. Henry was even more surprised when he saw what Scooter was holding—a real cowhide football stitched with nylon thread and laced with real buckskin thongs!

"Hi, Scoot," said Henry. "Boy oh boy! Where did you get that football?"

"My grandmother sent it to me for my birthday," answered Scooter.

"Your grandmother!" Henry could hardly believe it. "My grandmother sends me sweaters and socks."

"My grandmother sends me keen presents. Come on out and throw some passes with me."

Scooter pounded the football with his fist. It made a drumlike sound.

Henry could hardly wait to touch the leather. When the boys, followed by Ribsy, went out to the sidewalk, Scooter ran up the street a way and threw the ball back to Henry. It hit some branches that overhung the sidewalk but Henry caught it anyway. The ball felt just right. It was big and solid and smelled of new leather. Henry lovingly ran his hands over its surface before he sent it sailing back to Scooter. The ball hit the branch again.

"I know what," said Scooter. "If I went on the other side of the street and we threw it back and forth across the street, we wouldn't hit the trees." He tucked the ball under his arm as if he were running ninety yards for a touchdown and sprinted across the street.

Pow! The ball sailed into Henry's hands. It made a deep hollow sound, just the kind of sound a good football should make. Henry sent it back across the street. *Pow!* Scooter caught it. Back and forth the ball flew until Henry's hands began to tingle from the smack of leather against them.

"Throw it to me once more," called Scooter, "and then let's go down to the empty lot and practice kicking."

Henry wished he could carry the ball, but after all it did belong to Scooter. He gripped it firmly and drew it back over his shoulder. This time he was going to throw a perfect pass, the kind he had seen All-Americans make in newsreels.

As he started to bring his arm forward, Ribsy gave a sudden bark. Henry looked around at Ribsy, but his arm kept on going. The ball left his fingers.

At that instant a car whizzed around the corner. Scooter yelled, "Hey! Look out!"

It was too late. There was nothing Henry could do. The speeding car did not slow down, and for one terrible moment he thought the ball was going to hit the driver. Instead it sailed into the rear window, bounced against the closed window on the other side of the car, and then fell inside. The car raced on down the street and screeched around a corner on two wheels.

The football was gone!

The boys stared after the car. Henry was so surprised he stood there with his arm in the air. When he finally remembered to bring it down, he was still speechless.

"My football!" exclaimed Scooter. He stopped looking down the street after the departed car. He looked at Henry. "My ball is in that car," he said accusingly.

"Yeah, I guess it is." Henry was uncomfortable. "Maybe the man in the car will bring it back in a little while," he said hopefully.

"He'd better," said Scooter grimly.

The boys sat down on the curb to wait.

"Boy, I bet he was going eighty miles an hour!" said Henry.

"I couldn't even see his license plates."

"He ought to be arrested," said Henry, who was anxious to talk about anything but Scooter's football.

"He might kill somebody," said Scooter.

The boys waited and waited. The longer they waited, the more angry Scooter looked. "I don't think that car is going to come back," he said finally. "It's all your fault. You threw the ball."

"Yes, I know," admitted Henry, "but it wasn't my fault that Ribsy barked and that old car came by just then."

"You shouldn't have thrown it." Scooter scowled darkly.

"I couldn't help it." Henry scowled back. "I didn't even see the car until after I threw the ball. I couldn't catch it after I had thrown it, could I?"

"I don't care! You would have heard the car coming if that dumb dog of yours hadn't made so much noise. He wasn't even barking at anything. You lost my new ball and you're going to have to buy me a new one. If you don't I'll—I'll . . ." Scooter wasn't quite sure what he would do, so he didn't finish the sentence.

Henry didn't know what to say. It did not seem right that he was to blame. Still, half an hour ago Scooter had a new football. Now it was gone and Henry had been the last one to touch it.

"I have forty-six cents and three milk bottles you could have," said Henry hopefully. He hated to see that football disappear almost as much as Scooter did.

"That isn't enough," said Scooter. "You'll have to buy me a new football before next Saturday or

I'll tell my dad and he'll tell your dad and then you'll really get it."

Henry suspected Scooter was right. He probably would get it. Once when he had accidentally broken another boy's roller skate, his father had given him a talking to and then made him spend his allowance to have it fixed. "O.K." he said. "I'll get you a new football. I don't know how but I guess I'll manage."

Henry turned and went slowly into the house. Ribsy followed him. "Now see what you've done," Henry said. "And after I spent my football money for your license and your collar and your dish, too." Ribsy hung his head.

Now Henry was just twice as far from owning a real cowhide football with nylon stitching and buckskin lacings as he had been half an hour ago. He was quiet the rest of the afternoon and all through dinner. He was thinking.

"How about another piece of gingerbread?" his father asked.

"No, thank you," said Henry absent-mindedly. "May I be excused, please?"

"Why, Henry, don't you feel well?" Mrs. Huggins was surprised. Henry usually ate two pieces of gingerbread and a third if she let him.

"Oh sure, I feel all right," said Henry and went out to sit on the front steps. Ribsy lay on the step below and dozed with his head on Henry's foot.

"Good old Ribsy, even if you did get me into trouble," said Henry.

He listened to the whish-click, whish-click of the water sprinkler next door and wondered how he was going to earn thirteen dollars and ninety-five cents in one week. He thought and thought.

He could collect old tin foil. No, that would take too long. Junk men didn't want the little wads of tin foil that came from old cigarette packs. They wanted big pieces that were too hard to find.

Maybe he could ask the neighbors for old papers and magazines. No, he had already collected all he could find for a school paper drive the week before. Besides, the junk men paid only half a cent a pound.

He could open a lemonade stand by the park, but lemonade stands were just kid stuff. Mothers and fathers were the only people who really spent any money for lemonade.

He could charge fifty cents for mowing lawns. That would be a dollar for two lawns. He would have to mow twenty-eight lawns to earn thirteen dollars and ninety-five cents. Even if he could get twenty-eight lawns to mow, he didn't see how he could find time after school.

As the evening grew darker, Henry still sat on the steps thinking and listening to the whish-click, whish-click of the water sprinkler. Whish-click, whish-click. Then Mr. Hector Grumbie, who lived next door, came out of the house and shut off the water. Henry liked Mr. Grumbie but he wasn't so sure about Mrs. Grumbie. She sprinkled Doggie-B-Gone on her shrubbery, and Ribsy disliked the smell very much.

Henry noticed that Mr. Grumbie had a flashlight in one hand and a quart fruit jar in the other. Mr. Grumbie set the jar on the sidewalk, tiptoed onto the lawn, flashed his light on the grass, bent over, and pounced on something. Then he picked it up and put it into the jar. It was too dark for Henry to see what it was.

The next time Mr. Grumbie pounced, he didn't put anything into the jar. Henry heard him mutter, "Oops, that one got away."

Henry couldn't stand it any longer. He had to know what Mr. Grumbie was doing. He walked across his own lawn and peered over the rosebushes.

"If you come any closer," said Mr. Grumbie, "you'd better tiptoe. I don't want to scare them away."

"Scare what away?" asked Henry.

"Night crawlers," said Mr. Grumbie.

"Night crawlers!" exclaimed Henry. "What are night crawlers?"

"Worms," said Mr.
Grumbie. "Great big
worms. Do you mean
to say you've lived
here all these years and never seen a night
crawler?"

"No, I haven't," answered Henry. "How big are
they?"

"Oh, about seven to ten inches long."

"Golly!" Henry could hardly believe it. "Ten
inches long! I didn't know worms came that big."

"Here's one." Mr. Grumbie swooped and held
up a worm in the beam of his flashlight. It was a
big fat worm. It was at least nine inches long and
as big around as a pencil.

"Wow!" said Henry. It was hard to believe, but
there it was. Mr. Grumbie put it into the jar.

"Do you use them to catch fish?" asked Henry.

"That's right." Mr. Grumbie pounced again.

"What kind of fish?"

"Some kinds of trout, salmon, perch, catfish—

different kinds of fish. I'm going salmon fishing in the Columbia River in the morning."

Henry thought this over. "Do you always catch worms at night?"

"Yes. They only come out at night when the ground is wet. I give the lawn a good soaking so they'll come up to the top. Then I turn on the light and grab them quick before they have a chance to pull back into the ground."

Mrs. Grumbie stepped out on the porch and called to her husband. "Hector, if you expect me to have a lunch ready for you to take fishing at three o'clock in the morning, you'd better go to the store for a loaf of bread right now before it closes."

"All right. In a minute." As his wife went back into the house, Mr. Grumbie said to Henry, "How would you like to earn some money?"

"Catching worms? I'll say I would!"

"I'll pay you a penny apiece for every night crawler you catch."

"Golly," said Henry. "A penny apiece! How many do you want?"

"As many as you can catch. If I can't use them, some of the other men can." He handed Henry the jar and the flashlight, got into his car, and drove away.

A penny apiece! There were one hundred pennies in a dollar, so it would take one thousand three hundred and ninety-five worms to pay for the football. And forty-one worms for the tax!

Henry went around the rosebushes and tiptoed across the grass. Because of the Doggie-B-Gone, Ribsy stayed on his own side of the rosebushes. Henry turned on the flashlight and sure enough, there on the grass was the end of a big fat worm. But when Henry bent to pick it up, it was gone.

He tiptoed farther across the grass and turned on the light again. This time he moved faster. He grabbed the end of the cold slippery worm. The other end was already in the ground. Henry pulled and the worm pulled. The worm stretched. It grew longer and thinner until it snapped out of Henry's hand and disappeared into the ground.

"Ugh!" said Henry.

The next time he moved still faster. He pounced on the worm before either end had a chance to get in the ground. He caught it! That's one penny, he thought.

After that it was easier. He caught most of the worms on the first pounce. Pretty soon he had caught sixty-two worms. Then he discovered he was running out of worms. Either he had caught all of Mr. Grumbie's worms or they had felt him walking around on the ground and had retired for the night. And he hadn't earned enough to pay for the football.

Just as Henry was wondering where he could find more worms, Mr. Grumbie came back from the store. "I caught sixty-two worms for you," said Henry.

"Sixty-two! That's great!" Mr. Grumbie reached into his pants pocket and brought out a handful of change. He picked out a fifty-cent piece, a dime, and two pennies and gave them to Henry.

"Thank you," said Henry politely. He wished he had caught more worms.

Mr. Grumbie started to go into the house and then stopped. "Say, Shorty," he said to Henry, who was going back through the rosebushes, "I'll tell you what you can do. Sunday morning I'm going fishing with a bunch of men from my lodge. Quite a few of us are going and we can use all the worms you can catch. Tomorrow night you get someone to help you and catch enough for all of us."

"Sure," said Henry eagerly. "I'll catch hundreds of worms for you."

"Swell! We can use them," answered Mr. Grumbie as he went into the house.

Henry sat down on his front steps again. Because he needed so much money, he knew he would have to catch all the worms himself. That meant he would need a lot of wet lawn. His mother would be pleased, even surprised, to have him water the lawn, but his lawn and the Grumbies' lawn wouldn't be enough. Maybe he could ask all the people on the street to water their yards Saturday evening. However, if he did that, Beezus and Robert and the other kids would ask what he was doing. Henry was afraid they would want to earn money catching worms, too. He knew Beezus would want to. She was the kind of girl who would like catching worms.

Henry sat on the steps wishing he had acres and acres of wet lawn. He thought and thought about millions of wet green blades of grass with big fat worms peeping out from under them. The park! Of course, that was it! It was only a few blocks away and because September had been unusually warm this year, the grass in the park was watered every day. If his mother would let him stay up later than nine o'clock, he knew he could catch enough worms to pay for the football.

Henry went into the living room where his mother was knitting an Argyle sock.

"Mom, could I stay up later tomorrow night?" Henry told his mother the whole story.

Mrs. Huggins put down the sock. "Henry," she sighed, "how do you manage to get yourself into such messes?"

"Well, gee," said Henry, "I didn't do anything. I just threw this football and . . ."

"Yes, you told me," his mother interrupted. "Yes, you may stay up tomorrow night, but for goodness' sake, Henry, after this do be careful with other people's belongings."

Saturday was an anxious day for Henry. He wanted to avoid Scooter, but he also wanted to go to the park to make sure the grass was being watered. Unfortunately, he had to pass Scooter's house to reach the park. He walked on the other side of the street, but Scooter was in his front yard tightening the chain on his bicycle.

He shook his fist at Henry and yelled, "You get me that ball or I'll fix you!"

"You and who else?" Henry yelled back and

kept on going. When he reached the park he was relieved to hear the swish of the sprinklers and see water spraying over the grass. He would earn thirteen dollars and ninety-five cents before he went to bed that night.

That evening Henry didn't wait for dessert. He borrowed his father's flashlight and several old mayonnaise jars and ran down the hill to the park. It was a warm night and the tennis courts and swimming pool were floodlighted. It was only beginning to get dark, but Henry hoped it might be dark enough under the bushes to start catching worms. He couldn't afford to waste time.

He passed the playground where he heard the children's shouts and the clank and clang of the rings and swings. Henry didn't stop. He had work to do. He went to the edge of the park where there were no lights and turned on his flashlight. Sure enough, there in the grass under a bush was a night crawler. Henry nabbed it and put it into his jar. Then he caught another. He caught worm after worm. Four hundred thirty-one, four hundred thirty-two, four hundred thirty-three. Henry was tired of pouncing. Henry was tired of worms.

When the lights of the swimming pool went off, Henry was still working. By the time that the lights at the tennis courts went off, Henry was very, very tired of worms. But he kept on. When he had added the one thousand one hundred and third worm to his collection he heard someone calling, "Henry! Henry! Where are you?" It was his mother.

"Here I am." As Henry stood up to rest his aching back, he saw his mother and father walking along the path.

"My goodness, Henry," Mrs. Huggins exclaimed. "Haven't you caught those worms yet? You can't stay out in the park alone all night."

"But Mom, I don't have enough worms to pay for Scooter's football. And I promised to get him a new one this week. I have one thousand one hundred and three worms and I need to catch one thousand three hundred and thirty-one altogether. I had some money saved and I earned some last night."

"Let's see. He needs two hundred and twenty-eight more. It shouldn't take long to catch them," Mr. Huggins said to Mrs. Huggins. "After all, he promised. Let's help him."

So Henry and his mother and father bent and pounced together. Henry felt a little uncomfortable to see his mother catching worms, but he was very, very glad when the one thousand three hundred and thirty-first worm was in the jar. He took his jars of worms to Mr. Grumbie, who paid him thirteen dollars and thirty-one cents. As Henry watched him turn the night crawlers into a box of dirt so they would live until Sunday, he thought he never wanted to see another worm.

He felt the money in his pocket. "I guess this ought to take care of old Scooter," he said and, wishing he could spend it on a football for himself, he went home to bed.

Sunday morning Henry lay on his stomach on the living-room floor reading the funny papers. Usually he woke up early and read the funnies before his mother and father were awake, but this morning he was so tired from catching worms that he slept later than usual.

The doorbell rang and Mr. Huggins, who was reading the sports section and drinking coffee, put down his paper and answered the door.

Henry heard a strange man ask, "Excuse me, could you tell me who owns this football?"

Henry didn't wait for his father to answer. He ran to the door.

The man was holding Scooter's real cowhide football, stitched with nylon thread and laced with buckskin thongs!

"Golly!" said Henry. "That's the football I lost for Scooter McCarthy."

The man handed it to Henry. "I'm sorry I couldn't stop when the ball landed in my car. I had to take my wife to the hospital in a hurry. I would have returned it sooner, but I couldn't leave the kids."

"That's O.K.," said Henry. "Gee, thanks for bringing it back."

When the man had gone, Henry showed the football to his father. "See, Dad," he said, "this is the kind of football I'm going to buy with my night crawler money." Then he tucked the football under his arm as if he were running ninety yards for a touchdown and sprinted down the street to Scooter's house.

CHAPTER FOUR

The Green
Christmas

HENRY was glad he sat in the row by the windows in Room Four, because he could watch for snowflakes. Even though his father said they would probably have a green Christmas this year, Henry still hoped for snow. He was pretty sure the package hidden behind some boxes in the garage was the sled he wanted, a real Flexible Flyer.

While he sat at his desk looking out at the clouds for signs of snow, he was listening to Miss Roop talk about the Christmas operetta and thinking he had taken part in enough school plays for one semester.

In September he had been Second Indian in a

play for the Westward Expansion Unit. That hadn't been too bad. He had stuck an old feather out of a duster in his hair and worn an auto robe his mother let him take to school. It was an easy part, because all he had to say

was "Ugh!" First Indian and Third Indian also said "Ugh!" It really hadn't mattered which Indian said "Ugh!" Once all three said it at the same time.

Then in November Robert came down with mumps just be-fore Book Week. At the last minute Henry had to wear a long cotton beard and read Robert's part, one of the seven dwarfs in a play called "Storyland Favorites Come to Life." It was not a play that appealed to Henry, but

at least he did not have to memorize any lines or do much practicing, because there wasn't time. During the performance he had to stop reading several times in order to take pieces of his beard out of his mouth.

His worst part had been in a Parent Teacher program for National Brush Your Teeth Week. Henry had been really disgusted that day. He had to wear his best trousers and a white shirt to school and he had to stay clean all day. Then he missed practicing with his football, because the meeting was after school. Worst of all, he had to stand up in front of all the mothers and teachers, bow, and recite:

> I am Sir Cuspid,
> My job is to bite.
> Brush me twice daily
> To keep me so white.

The kids called him Sir Cuspidor for a long time after that.

Now Miss Roop was telling the class that the Christmas operetta was called "A Visit to Santa Claus." It was about a mother and father and their two children who visited Santa Claus at the North Pole on Christmas Eve. Henry thought it was a dumb play. In the end it turned out that the little boy had dreamed the whole thing. Henry disliked stories that ended by being someone's dream.

Miss Roop said, "Since the whole school is giving the operetta, there won't be parts for everyone in our room."

That's good, thought Henry. He slid way down in his seat so Miss Roop wouldn't notice him when she assigned parts.

Miss Roop continued. "Richard, Arthur, Ralph, and David will be four of Santa Claus's reindeer. The other four will be chosen from Room Five." So far Henry was safe! He stayed down in his seat just to be sure. "Mary Jane, you are to have the part of the Dancing Doll. Beezus—uh, I mean Beatrice, you will be the Rag Doll." Girls' parts. Henry felt a little safer. "Robert, you will be the Big Brown Dog," Miss Roop went on. All the children laughed.

"Gr-r-r-r. Arf! Arf!" said Robert. The children laughed again.

When Miss Roop started to hand out the parts, Henry decided she had come to the end of the list. He sat up straight in his seat and looked out of the window at the sky. It looked darker. There might be snow before Christmas after all. He was glad he wouldn't have to stay in after school to rehearse "A Visit to Santa Claus." He wanted to make snow men and throw snowballs, since, of course, his mother and father would not give him the Flexible Flyer until Christmas. When he had his sled, he wanted to coast on the Thirty-third Street hill.

Miss Roop, holding one part in her hand, stood in front of the class again and smiled in Henry's direction. Just in case she was smiling at him, Henry quickly slid down in his seat again.

She *was* smiling at him. She said, "And the best part of all goes to Henry Huggins. Henry, you are the shortest boy in Room Four, so you are to have the part of Timmy, the little boy who dreams the whole story." The class shouted with laughter.

A little boy! It was worse than anything Henry had imagined. He could never live down the part of a little boy! Sir Cuspid had been bad enough, but a little boy—the kids would never stop teasing him. "Miss Roop," he said desperately, "there're lots of littler kids in the lower grades. Couldn't one of them have the part?"

"No, Henry. All the second and third grade boys are needed for the chorus of polar bears and the first grade boys are too little to learn so many lines." She handed Henry his part. So many carbons had been typed at one time that the thin paper was almost too blurry to read.

Henry made out:

ACT I. The scene is Timmy's bedroom. Timmy is wearing pajamas. Enter Timmy's mother.

TIMMY'S MOTHER: Hurry up and get into bed, Timmy. This is Christmas Eve and good little boys should be asleep when Santa Claus comes.

TIMMY: Yes, Mother. (Timmy gets into bed. His mother tucks him in and kisses him good night.)

TIMMY'S MOTHER: Good night, Timmy. Pleasant dreams. (Goes out and shuts door.)

TIMMY: Ho hum. My, I am sleepy! I wonder what Santa Claus will have for me in his pack. I think—I—will—try—to—stay—awake. (Falls asleep.)

Henry groaned. It was even worse than he had expected. Pajamas! Good-night kiss! Did they think he was going to stand up there on the stage in front of all the girls in the school in his pajamas? And be kissed by some dumb old eighth grade girl who was supposed to be his mother? It was horrible even to think about.

He had to find a way out! Already Robert was whispering across the aisle, "Hey, Little Boy!"

Henry ignored him. Maybe if he did stretching exercises for a whole hour every morning he would grow fast enough to outgrow the part. No, that wouldn't work. There wasn't time. He would have to think of something else.

During the rest of the afternoon Henry had trouble keeping his mind on Social Studies. He was too busy trying to find a way out of playing Timmy, the Little Boy. When the last bell rang, he grabbed his beanie and raincoat from the cloakroom. He was first out of Room Four and first out of the school building.

Ribs was waiting under the fir tree out of the rain. "Come on, Ribsy," Henry yelled, "let's keep ahead of the rest of the kids!"

But he wasn't quite fast enough. Beezus and Robert and Scooter were right behind him. "Hi there, Timmy!" they yelled. "How's the Little Boy?" Then they began to chant, "Henry is a Little Boy! Henry is a Little Boy!"

Henry slowed down. "Aw, shut up!" he yelled back. "You think you're smart, but you're not. You're just an old Rag Doll and a Brown Dog. And I'll bet Scooter is something dumb, too!"

"You wouldn't catch me being in any old operetta," said Scooter loftily. "I'm on the stage crew. I get to pull the curtain and turn on the lights and paint the scenery and stuff."

Mary Jane came skipping down the street, jumping across the puddles on the sidewalk. "Here comes the old Dancing Doll!" yelled Henry.

"Yes." Mary Jane smiled proudly. "I'll wear my new ballet slippers and my pink taffeta party dress and have my hair curled."

The other children were disappointed. They couldn't tease Mary Jane if she wanted to be a Dancing Doll. It gave Henry an idea. He waited until Scooter said, "I'll bet the Little Boy will look real cute in his pajamas. Are you going to wear the kind with feet in them, Little Boy?"

"Aw, you're just jealous because you don't have an important part like I have. I have the most important part in the whole operetta!"

"Don't be funny!" Scooter laughed. "I wouldn't learn all those lines and run around in front of a

bunch of people in my pajamas for a million tril-
lion dollars!"

It was a good idea but it didn't work. Henry
would have to think of something else. Maybe he
could pretend to be sick. No, that wouldn't do.
His mother would make him go to bed and if it
did happen to snow, he would have to stay in
the house while all the other children were out
sliding on the Thirty-third Street hill.

By the time Henry reached his house on Klickitat Street, he decided to say nothing about the
operetta to his mother and father until he could
work things out. He said hello to his mother, who
was writing a letter on the typewriter, and then he
went into the kitchen to fix himself a snack of
peanut butter, jam, and pickle relish on graham
crackers. He spread a cracker with peanut butter
and gave it to Ribsy. Then he leaned against the
refrigerator to munch and think.

Tap-tap-tap went the typewriter. Henry fixed
himself another cracker. Tap-tap-tap. He heard

his mother pull the sheet of paper out of the machine. Then he heard her go into the bedroom. The typewriter—that was it!

"Hey, Mom, can I use the typewriter?"

"*May* I use the typewriter."

"May I use the typewriter?" asked Henry patiently.

"Yes, Henry, but don't pound too hard."

Henry gulped down his graham cracker with peanut butter, jam, and pickle relish. He wiped his fingers on the seat of his jeans and went into the living room. There he sat down at the desk, took a sheet of paper from the drawer, and put it into the typewriter. He thought a while and then began to type. He didn't make the typewriter go tap-tap-tap the way his mother did. He made only one tap at a time and then, after a long pause while he looked for the right letter, he made another tap. He had to remind himself to push the extra key to make capital letters.

Henry worked a long time. Fortunately his

mother did not pay any attention to his typing.
Tap. Tap. Tap. At last it was finished. Henry
pulled the paper out of the typewriter and read:

dEar mIss rrOOP?
  P½easee xcuze henry from the ~~oppar~~ φφàff Play/
HE Has to mucj workk todo at home¢.

MRs, hUggins

Somehow it didn't look the way he had thought
it would. The capitals were not in the right places.
He knew *much* wasn't spelled with a *j* or *yours*
with a *z*. His fingers had just put themselves on
the wrong keys. Henry tore his letter into little
pieces and threw them in the fireplace. He ran
another piece of paper into the typewriter and
started again. Tap. Tap. Tap. When the second
letter was finished, it read:

DEar inisS rOop.
P PLease ezcude Henry Fro m the play? eH has
φφφ too much wwork too   doat home.

YYours turly/
        mRs, hUggins

Henry studied it. Those capitals again. He pushed the thing too soon or not soon enough. And who ever heard of a word like *ezcude*? Or *doat*? His fingers just didn't hit the right keys. No, the letter was not a finished product. Henry tore this one up, too, and threw it in the fireplace. He would have to think of something else.

When rehearsals started after school the next day, Henry still had not thought of a way out.

Miss Roop said that today the children would read their parts, but by next week they must have them memorized. "Henry, you and Alice are on the stage first," she directed. Alice was the eighth grade girl who was to play the part of Timmy's mother. "Come on, Henry, don't waste time."

Henry slouched up the steps to the stage. He pulled his crumpled part out of his hip pocket and looked at it. He decided to pretend he couldn't read it. Maybe if he read everything wrong, Miss Roop would give someone else the part.

Alice read, "Hurry up and get into bed, Timmy. This is Christmas Eve and good little boys should be asleep when Santa Claus comes."

Henry held the paper almost against his nose. He frowned and squinted. He didn't say, "Yes, Mother." He said, after scowling and twisting the paper around, "Yeah, Ma."

"Henry Huggins!" Miss Roop interrupted. "You read what is typed on that paper!"

"Well, gee whiz, Miss Roop, it's so blurry I can hardly see what it says."

"Bring your part to me."

Henry slouched off the stage and handed it to her. "Now Henry, it isn't as blurred as all that. However, since you have such a long part you had better trade with me."

Well, that's that, thought Henry. None of his ideas seemed to work.

"Continue," ordered Miss Roop.

The operetta proceeded. It seemed to Henry that it took a long time to go through it. The music teacher played the music for the songs they were supposed to learn by next week. Henry discovered that in the second act he was supposed to stand in the center of the stage and sing a song all by himself. It went:

Hurrah for Santa! Hurrah for Saint Nick!
He comes from the North with reindeer and sleigh,
Riding on clouds up high in the sky
With a pack full of toys so children can play.

It was the dumbest song Henry had ever heard. Hurrah for Santa! It was just plain stupid. He felt a little better when he learned that Robert had to sing an even dumber song called "Woof, Woof, I'm a Big Brown Dog."

As Christmas drew near, Henry became more and more discouraged. Everybody in Glenwood School called him Little Boy. His mother and father found out about his part in the play, because Mary Jane told her mother and she told Henry's mother. He had to learn his lines and recite them every evening while his father looked at the part and prompted him. He scarcely had time to go out to the garage to peek at the Flexible Flyer package.

Mrs. Huggins went downtown to buy him a pair of new pajamas to wear in the first act. They were made of pink-and-blue-and-white-striped flannel. Henry felt that any pajamas were bad enough— but pink-and-blue pajamas! He didn't even like to think about them.

Henry swallowed hard every morning. He hoped his throat might be a little bit sore but it never was. Finally he gave up. There was no way out. Now all he wanted was to get it over.

One afternoon during fifth period Henry looked out of the window and saw a few feathery snow-flakes drifting down. They were so light he wasn't sure at first. When Miss Roop wasn't looking, he leaned over closer to the window. It was snow, all right! It wasn't going to be a green Christmas after all! Now he would get to use his Flexible Flyer!

The rest of the class soon noticed the snow too, and everyone began to whisper. Miss Roop smiled and pretended not to hear. As soon as the bell rang, the children all scrambled for their wraps and rushed out to see the snow—all except those who had parts in the operetta. They took their wraps from the cloakroom and went to the auditorium.

The auditorium was a busy place. In one corner of the room, mothers from the Parent Teacher Association were altering costumes for the polar bear chorus. Henry remembered those white suits. He had worn one when he had been an Easter

bunny in a spring program. Now the mothers were ripping off the long ears and fuzzy tails, and were sewing on short ears and straight tails to change the suits into polar bear costumes.

The stage crew was at work. Some of the eighth grade boys were turning different-colored lights on and off. At the back of the stage, Scooter, standing on a board laid across two stepladders, was painting scenery with green paint.

Henry sat down to wait for his turn, while Mary Jane and Beezus rehearsed their dance, and Robert, wearing his dog suit, practiced walking on all fours.

Henry waited and waited. He sat on the hard auditorium chair and looked out of the window at the snowflakes. He could hear the other kids laughing and yelling outside, so he knew there must be enough snow for snowballs. He wished his turn would come so he could leave. Now the tin soldiers were practicing their steps. At the end of their song and dance one of the stage crew threw a basketball across the stage in front of them. It was supposed to look like a cannon ball, and the tin soldiers were supposed to fall over with one leg in the air. Miss Roop didn't like the way they fell and she made them do it over several times.

Henry wandered up on the stage behind the tin soldiers to watch Scooter paint scenery. "What're you supposed to be painting?" he asked him.

"Trees," answered Scooter. "With real paint."

"Where did you get it?"

"A fellow in my room's father has a paint store and he gave it to us."

Just then Henry heard a bark. It sounded like Ribsy. It *was* Ribsy. He bounded in through the door of the auditorium, ran up the steps to the stage, and wormed his way behind the row of tin soldiers to get to Henry. He shook himself and wagged his tail.

"Well, Ribsy, old boy!" said Henry. "Did you get tired of waiting out in the cold?" Ribsy shook himself again. Henry patted him. "Why, Ribs. you're all wet! It must be snowing hard."

"He's a dumb-looking dog," said Scooter.

"Aw, he is not. He's a smart dog. Aren't you, Ribsy?"

"I'll bet he can't climb a stepladder like my dog can," said Scooter.

"I'll bet he can. Call him and see."

Scooter looked down at the dog. "Here, Ribsy," he called. "Come on, boy." Ribsy looked at him and then at Henry.

"Go on," said Henry. "Up the ladder." He pointed to the ladder. Ribsy put one paw on the bottom step. "Atta boy, go on!" Ribsy carefully put a paw on the next step. "Good dog!" said Henry, urging him on.

"Come on, Ribsy," coaxed Scooter. Ribsy cautiously made his way up to the board on top of the stepladders.

"Good old Ribsy!" said Henry. "See, I told you he could do it!"

Pleased with himself, Ribsy looked down at his master, wagged his tail, and said, "Woof!"

"You be quiet!" ordered Henry in a loud whisper. "If Miss Roop hears you, she'll throw you out!"

Ribsy sat down on the board and looked around the auditorium.

"Beat it!" said Scooter. "Can't you see I have work to do?"

"Here, Ribsy!" whispered Henry. "You don't want Miss Roop to see you, do you?"

Ribsy liked sitting on the board.

"See, I told you he was a dumb dog." Scooter picked up his can of paint and stepped over Ribsy. He set the can down and went on painting treetops.

"Come on, Ribsy!"

"Aw, he's too dumb to go down the ladder."

"He is not! Here, Ribsy!"

Ribsy stood up and sniffed at the can of paint. "Here, Ribsy! Come on down," begged Henry, looking up at his dog. "Come on, you old dog. I'll catch it if Miss Roop sees you."

Miss Roop clapped her hands for attention,

the music ceased, and the tin soldiers stopped falling down.

"How did that dog get in here?" she demanded.

"I don't know," answered Henry. "I guess he just walked in."

"Well, take him out!"

Henry did not move.

"Quickly, Henry! We have a lot to do this afternoon."

"Gee whiz, Miss Roop, I'm trying to take him out but he won't come down."

"I'll carry him down, Miss Roop," offered Scooter. "I don't think he knows how to go down a ladder."

Henry glared at Scooter.

"No, he's too heavy to carry down a ladder. You might fall," said Miss Roop.

Just then Ribsy sat down to scratch behind his left ear. Thump. Thump. Thump. His hind leg bumped against the can of paint. The can tipped. Scooter yelled. Ribsy barked.

"Henry! Look out!" screamed Miss Roop.

The can fell over and green paint poured down over Henry.

"Glub!" said Henry as he heard Miss Roop run up onto the stage. He heard her but he couldn't see her. He had to keep his eyes shut. The cold, oily paint was dribbling down his face and neck. He could feel it dripping off his ears.

Miss Roop made a squeaking noise. Then Henry could feel her rubbing his head with something made of cloth.

"Run and get some paper towels!" she called to the other children. She wiped away at his face. "I knew I shouldn't have let those boys use real paint. They should have used poster paint. It would have washed off. Oh dear, I'm afraid your shirt is ruined."

Henry heard Ribsy barking. When he could see again he found all the tin soldiers and polar bears and P.T.A. mothers crowded around him. Miss Roop began to scrub his hair with paper towels. "Oh, that's all right," he said to Miss Roop. "It's an old shirt anyway." The towels she was wiping him with felt scratchy on his ears and neck.

Ribsy continued to bark and to pace back and forth across the board as he looked down at his master.

"Quiet, Ribsy!" ordered Henry.

Ribsy stopped barking and looked anxiously at the floor. Then he looked at Henry. Before Henry realized what was happening, Ribsy leaped from the board, sailed over the heads of several tin soldiers and polar bears, and landed on all fours in the puddle of paint. He skidded and sat down.

"Ribsy!" groaned Henry. Then he said to Scooter, "See, he was smart enough to get down by himself."

The dog began to bark and run around Henry. He left a circle of green footprints on the floor of the stage.

"Oh, Henry," wailed Miss Roop and then said sharply, "Scooter, take that dog out of the building! And carry him. I don't want any green footprints in the halls!"

"Yes, Miss Roop." Scooter lugged the barking dog away.

Mary Jane squirmed through the crowd to look at Henry. "Henry Huggins!" she exclaimed. "Wait till your mother sees you! Your hair is green and so is your skin!"

Beezus laughed. "Henry, your face looks just like a green apple!"

"Henry, I'm afraid this isn't going to come off for a long time," said Miss Roop.

Someone handed Henry a mirror. "Golly!" breathed Henry. He stared into the mirror. His hair and eyebrows were pale green. His face was all green at the forehead and streaked with green toward his chin. His ears were green all over. "Jeepers! Green ears!" He couldn't take his eyes off the mirror. Secretly he thought he looked fascinating. Like a leprechaun in a fairy tale. Now maybe the kids would stop calling him Little Boy! That gave him an idea.

"Miss Roop, I can't be in the operetta when I'm all green, can I?" he asked hopefully.

Miss Roop sighed. "No, Henry, I guess you can't." She looked at him. Then she smiled. "I'll give your part to someone else and you can play the part of the Green Elf! Now run along home."

The Green Elf! That was a good part. The Green Elf turned somersaults and didn't have to say anything.

Henry put on his raincoat and beanie and went out into the snow. It was deep enough to scrunch under his feet. He scooped up a handful and threw it at Ribsy, who was waiting under the fir tree. The snow would be just right for coasting on the Thirty-third Street hill when his mother and father surprised him with the Flexible Flyer at Christmas. In the meantime he would make a snow man on the front lawn. Maybe he would make a whole snow family. Even a snow dog.

"Good old Ribsy. I don't know how I'd ever get along without you." He took out his handkerchief and wiped green paint from his dog's tail.

Then Henry followed a set of big footprints in the snow. He took big steps and carefully put his feet into the marks someone else had made in the snow. "Jeepers!" he exclaimed. "I'm going to have a green Christmas and a white Christmas at the same time. Won't Mom be surprised?"

CHAPTER FIVE

The Pale
Pink Dog

WHEN Henry woke up one Monday morning in the spring, the first thing he thought was, Five more days till Saturday. On Tuesday the first thing he thought was, Four more days till Saturday. By Wednesday he felt as if Saturday would never come.

It all began when Henry and Ribsy made their weekly trip to the Lucky Dog Pet Shop to buy horse meat.

"Well, if it isn't Henry and Ribs!" exclaimed Mr. Pennycuff. "Do you have your entry blank for the dog show?"

"What dog show?" asked Henry.

"Didn't you hear? The park department is having a dog show in the park next Saturday. Boys and girls up to sixteen years old may enter their dogs. The Woofies Dog Food Company is giving prizes. Better take an entry blank and fill it out. A fine dog like Ribsy is sure to win a prize."

Ribsy wagged his tail.

"Well," said Henry doubtfully, "he's an awfully good dog but he isn't any special kind. I mean he isn't a cocker or bulldog or anything."

"That doesn't matter in this show. Now you just take this blank and fill it out. See, here's a place for dogs of mixed breed like Ribs."

"Gee, thanks," said Henry. "I think I will."

He took his entry blank and two pounds of horse meat, and he and Ribsy ran all the way home.

When they came to Klickitat Street, Henry saw Scooter and Robert playing catch. Mary Jane and Beezus and her little sister Ramona were standing under a snowball bush, shaking petals down

over themselves and pretending it was snowing.

"Hey, look!" yelled Henry, waving the paper at them.

The children gathered around him to look at his entry blank. "I'm going to enter Ribsy," said Henry. "He'll win a prize. Mr. Pennycuff said so."

"Aw, Ribsy's just an old mutt!" scoffed Scooter.

"He is not! He's a smart dog and besides, it says he doesn't have to be any special kind of dog. See, it says dogs of mixed breed."

"Say, look at the list of prizes!" said Robert. "Woofies Dog Food, squeaking mice, feeding dishes, leashes, movie tickets, beanies, silver loving cups—a whole lot of stuff."

"If they're giving silver cups, I'm going to get a blank for Princess Patricia of Tarabrook. She's a better dog than Ribsy," said Mary Jane.

"Princess who?" demanded Scooter.

"Princess Patricia of Tarabrook. That's Patsy's real name. She has a pedigree and I know she'll win a silver cup." Patsy was Mary Jane's cocker spaniel.

"You know," said Robert thoughtfully, "I'm going to enter Sassy. She's getting kind of old, but she's still pretty lively and she might win a movie ticket or something."

Beezus and Ramona didn't have a dog. They had a cat, three white rats, a turtle, and one guppy. Beezus said she knew where she could borrow a puppy named Puddles.

"Well, I guess I might as well enter Rags," said Scooter. "He's the smartest dog around here. He can even sit up and shake hands. And he's all Airedale, too. He isn't any mixed breed like that old mutt you found."

"Ribsy isn't old and he isn't a mutt either! And he can sit up, too. He's a better dog than your old Rags and he'll win a better prize. I'll bet he wins a silver cup!"

"Don't make me laugh!" scoffed Scooter. "If he'd been any good, his folks wouldn't have let him get away."

At last Saturday came. Henry jumped out of bed as soon as he woke up, because he had a lot to do before the dog show at ten o'clock. At breakfast he stopped gulping his cereal to ask, "Mom, can I give Ribsy a bath in the bathtub?"

"*May* I give Ribsy a bath in the bathtub."

"May I give Ribsy a bath in the bathtub?"

"Can't you use the laundry tub in the basement the way you usually do?" his mother asked.

"But, Mom, this is special for the dog show. I want to do an extra good job on him this time. If I get him good and clean, I know he'll win a silver cup."

Mrs. Huggins sighed. "Yes, Henry, you may

give Ribsy a bath in the bathtub if you'll promise to clean up the bathroom afterward."

"Thanks, Mom. I'll clean it up. Excuse me, please."

"Henry, I'm afraid you didn't eat much breakfast. I hope Ribsy does win a silver cup, but I wouldn't count on it too much if I were you. After all, he's just a mongrel."

"He isn't a mongrel, Mom. He's a mixed breed. And I know he's a better dog than any dog around here. Come on, Ribsy."

Ribsy followed Henry into the bathroom. When Henry began to run the water into the tub, he looked at Henry and then at the water. Then he tucked his tail between his legs and started to sneak out of the bathroom.

"Oh no you don't!" Henry grabbed him by the collar. He put his arms around Ribsy's middle and lifted him into the tub. Ribsy was heavier than he had been that day about a year ago when Henry carried him into the bus.

Because this was a special occasion, Henry didn't use flea soap. He used his mother's shampoo. Ribsy whimpered. Henry rubbed the shampoo on him and worked it into a thick lather. He rubbed and scrubbed. The suds foamed thick and white until Ribsy, except for his face, was hidden in mounds of thick lather.

"Now you ought to be good and clean," said Henry. He scooped up handfuls of water from the tub and poured them over the dog. He poured and poured but the lather only grew thicker. If only he hadn't used so much shampoo! He tried mopping Ribsy with his washcloth. That helped but it still wasn't fast enough. He had an idea. He moved Ribsy around so that he faced the end of the tub, and turned the shower on him. Ribsy tried to jump out but Henry held him. Ribsy raised his head and howled.

"Henry!" his mother called. "What are you doing to that poor dog?"

"Just washing him," answered Henry, and

turned off the shower. Ribsy shook himself. Henry used four bath towels on him, but still he wasn't dry.

Oh well, it's a warm day. Maybe the sun will dry him off, thought Henry. He took one of the towels and hastily wiped it over the floor and tub.

"Henry, I have to go downtown this morning. I hope you and Ribsy have good luck at the dog show." Mrs. Huggins had her hat on, ready to leave.

"Thanks, Mom. Say, have you seen the leash? It says on the entry blank all dogs must be on a leash."

"I think you left it in the basement," Mrs. Huggins said as she went out.

Henry ran down to the basement. At the bottom of the stairs he found the leash—at least, it had been a leash once. Now it was chewed into half a dozen pieces. Henry looked hurriedly around for something to use in its place. If only he had more time! The only thing he could find was his mother's rainy day clothesline. After climbing up on an apple box to untie it, he ran upstairs and fastened one end to Ribsy's collar. It was longer than a leash but it would have to do.

When Henry went out on the front porch, he saw Beezus and Ramona coming down the street. Beezus was carrying a squirming black puppy that kept trying to lick her face. "Puddles, you stop that!" she commanded and set him on the sidewalk. Puddles was wearing a red bow on his collar and Henry was pleased to see that Ribsy wasn't the only dog with a rope for a leash.

"Come on, Henry, we'd better hurry," said Beezus.

Ribsy sniffed at the puppy and decided to ignore him. "Hey, look," exclaimed Henry. "There's Mary Jane and Patsy and Robert and Sassy up there ahead. We'd better run."

When they reached the park, Henry saw that already there were hundreds of boys and girls and dogs there ahead of them. Henry had never seen so many dogs. There were boxers, Great Danes, Pekingese, Airedales, cockers, Saint Bernards, Pomeranians, beagles, setters, pointers, and just plain dogs. Some, like Puddles, were wearing ribbons on their collars, some wore sweaters, and some had on little paper hats.

A loud-speaker on a sound truck blared out. "Take your entry blanks to the registration desk by the tennis courts."

"Come on, Ribsy." Henry found his way through the crowds of children and dogs to the registration desk. There he waited in line to weigh Ribsy on a big scale. At first Ribsy didn't want to be weighed, but Henry and a boy scout managed to shove him upon the scale and keep him still long enough to see that he weighed twenty-eight pounds.

"You've grown a lot heavier in a year," said Henry. "Maybe we shouldn't call you Ribsy any more."

After the dog was weighed, a lady gave Henry a yellow cardboard arm band. It had "Woofies Dog Food—Woofies make dogs woof for joy" printed on it. Below that there was a space for the kind of dog, weight-class, and the ring in which the dog was to be shown. The lady wrote on it, "Mixed breed—25 to 40 pounds—Ring 3."

Henry led Ribsy toward a sign with "Ring 3"

printed on it over by a flower bed. Ribsy stopped to shake himself and then, before Henry knew what was happening, he dashed over to the flower bed and rolled in the dirt.

"Hey, cut that out!" yelled Henry. "You're getting all dirty."

It was too late. Henry pulled Ribsy, streaked with mud, out of the flowers. Henry tried to brush off the dirt. Then he tried to rub it off with his handkerchief. He only smeared it. He was discouraged. Why had he bragged so much about his dog? Now he would never win a prize.

When Henry reached Ring 3, he saw that it was made of rope tied to four stakes driven into

the ground. Inside was a table piled with the prizes Henry had read about. Henry looked at the silver cup and thought it would look nice on his dresser. Not that he had a chance with a muddy dog. He noticed some of the boys had brought brushes and were brushing their dogs. He wished he had thought to bring a brush.

The day was warm. Henry sat down on the grass with the rest of the boys and girls to wait for the judging to start. He kept trying to brush some of the dirt off Ribsy. In the ring next to his he saw a snow-white dog. Somebody said it was a Siberian sled dog. The dog's owner was brushing him and sprinkling white powder on him to make him look whiter.

Henry had an idea! If he only had time, he could run home for a can of talcum powder to sprinkle on the white parts of Ribsy! That would cover up the dirt. It didn't matter about the yellow and black and brown parts. The dirt didn't show there much.

Just then the voice boomed over the loud-speaker. "We are going to postpone the judging for a little while, because we have a real treat for all you kids. Maud, the trained mule, is going to entertain you."

The children all started toward the truck to see Maud. That is, all except Henry. He was not interested in any trained mule. He wanted Ribsy to win a silver cup. Here was his chance. He could run home and back while Maud the mule performed.

"Come on, Ribsy!" he yelled. "We have to step on it."

Followed by Ribsy, he ran as fast as he could out of the park and up the hill to his house on Klickitat Street. He rushed into his room and snatched his hairbrush. He tore into the bathroom and grabbed a can of talcum powder. Then he rushed back to the park with Ribsy. The children were still crowded around Maud.

Henry was so hot and sticky that he had to sit

down on the grass to catch his breath. Ribsy was panting and his tongue hung out. Henry brushed him with the hairbrush. That helped a little. Then he sprinkled powder on the big white spot on his back.

Henry was horrified. He could scarcely believe what he saw. The talcum powder wasn't white— it was pink! Who ever heard of a dog with pink spots! Quickly he tried to brush the powder off. But Ribsy was still damp and the powder didn't brush off.

Henry decided to make all Ribsy's white parts pink so they would match. Maybe in the bright sunshine the judges wouldn't notice. He sprinkled powder on Ribsy's white ear and left hind paw. He even sprinkled some on his white tail. Yes, Ribsy did look better with all his light parts matching. Maybe the judges would wear dark glasses.

Maud finished her act and the children came back to the rings with their dogs. "Hey, look at the pink dog!" a boy exclaimed.

"I never heard of a pink dog," a girl said. "What kind is he?"

"He's a mixed breed," said Henry.

He put the talcum powder can in his pocket and decided not to say anything about it. Maybe the others would think he had some rare breed of dog.

A man stood in the center of the ring. Henry noticed that he was not wearing dark glasses. "All right," the man called. "Bring your dogs into the ring and march them around in single file."

"Come on, Ribsy, they're going to start judging. You'd better behave yourself." Henry led him by the clothesline into the ring.

The children walked their dogs around in a circle. Ribsy's long rope tangled with the other dogs' leashes. Finally the judge directed them to stop. "Now get your dogs ready," he ordered.

Henry didn't know what he meant, so he watched the others. Some of them knelt by their dogs and made them stand still and look ahead.

That must be what the judge meant. Henry knelt beside Ribsy. Ribsy sat down. He opened his mouth and let his long pink tongue hang out. He was thirsty.

"Come on, Ribs, stand up," begged Henry. "Be a good dog." Ribsy began to pant. "Come on, get up!"

Ribsy lay down on the grass and panted harder. Henry pulled and tugged. He looked over his shoulder at the judge. The judge was looking at the ears and teeth of a dog that was standing properly. Then he ran his hands over the dog. The dog didn't move.

"Come on, Ribsy!" begged Henry. "It'll be our turn pretty soon." Ribsy closed his eyes. "I know you're thirsty. I'll get you a drink of water just as soon as I can."

The loud-speaker made an announcement. "Will the boy scouts please take pans of water to each ring?"

Henry was relieved to see a boy scout coming

with water, but when Ribsy's turn came, he sniffed at the pan and refused to drink.

"I guess he's used to his own dishes," explained Henry. "He just doesn't want to use the same pan as the other dogs."

"Can't help it," said the boy scout. "It's the only one I have."

Ribsy continued to pant.

At last the judge came to Henry. "Well, well, a pink dog," he exclaimed.

"Yes, sir," said Henry. It was lucky his own green hair had grown out so it could be cut off. A green-haired boy and a pale-pink dog would have looked funny.

"Come on, son. Stand him up."

Henry boosted Ribsy to his feet. Ribsy tried to sit down again, but Henry held up his hind end by the tail. The judge looked at his ears and teeth. Then he ran his hands over him. He looked at his fingers afterward. They were pink. "Hmmmm," he said.

When the judge had looked at all the dogs, he ordered each child to walk across the ring and back with his dog. Henry noticed that the boys and girls who knew about these things held the leash in the left hand. When his turn came he held the clothesline in his left hand and started across the ring. Halfway across, Ribsy sat down to scratch behind his left ear. Henry pulled at the rope. When he reached the other side of the ring and turned back, Ribsy turned the wrong way so that he crossed in front of Henry.

Henry tripped on the rope and started to change it to his right hand, but just then Ribsy ran around behind Henry to growl at a dog that was mostly spaniel. The boy who owned the spaniel pulled him away and started to the other side of the ring. Ribsy ran in front of Henry and pulled at his rope to get closer to the other dog. The harder he pulled, the tighter the rope drew around Henry's legs. The children began to laugh. Ribsy was so excited he ran around behind Henry and pulled the rope even tighter. The laughter increased.

"Cut that out, Ribsy!" Henry ordered, looking over his shoulder at his dog. He felt silly standing there wound up in a clothesline.

"Come on, son," said the judge. "We can't waste time. A lot of other boys and girls want to show their dogs, too."

Now, on top of all his troubles, the judge was cross with him. Henry knew a cross judge would never give him a silver cup. Discouraged and feeling even sillier, Henry twirled around like a top to unwind himself from the rope. Relieved to have that part of the show over, he dragged Ribsy to the side of the ring. In a few minutes he could take his dog home and give him a drink.

After each child had walked his dog, the judge went around the ring pointing to different boys and girls, saying, "All right, you stay in the ring." He looked at Henry and his dog. "Hmmmm," he said. "All right, you stay in."

As the contestants left the ring, the boy scouts

handed them prizes. Those who left first won the smallest prizes. The longer they stayed in the ring, the bigger the prize.

"Hey, Henry, are you still in?" Henry looked up. Robert and Sassy were standing outside the rope.

"Yes," answered Henry, "and I sure don't see why. Ribsy did everything wrong. Did Sassy win anything?"

"Just a dog whistle." Robert took another look at Ribsy. "Say, how did he get all pink?"

"Aw, mind your own beeswax," said Henry. He pretended to be watching the judge carefully. One by one the man asked the boys and girls to leave the ring.

"Look what I won!" Henry saw Beezus waving a rubber mouse. "See, it squeaks!" She squeaked it. Then she stopped. "Look!" she squealed. "Ribsy is pink!"

"Shut up!" Henry looked at the judge. He wished he knew why he was staying in the ring.

Every time the judge passed him he looked at Ribsy and said, "Hmmmm. Stay in the ring."

Mary Jane was the next one to see him. "See, I won a pillow for Patsy to sleep on," she said and then looked at Ribsy. "Why, Henry Huggins! What did you do to that poor dog? He's all pink. Just wait till your mother finds out about this."

"You keep quiet!" Henry said fiercely. There were only a few left in the ring.

Scooter was last to arrive. "Hi, Henry," he said. "Are you and that old mutt still in the ring? The judge must be blind. I guess Rags is a pretty good dog. Just the best in his class is all, and now he has to go to another ring to compete for the best dog in the show." He held up a small silver cup. Like the others, he looked at Ribsy. "I must be seeing things! A pink dog!" Scooter began to laugh. He sat down on the grass, laughing so hard he rolled back and forth.

Henry didn't think Ribsy was that funny. By this time Henry was so hot and disgusted that all he wanted was to get out of the ring, go home, and get Ribsy a drink of water out of his own private pan.

"Hmmmm," said the judge again. At last only Henry and another boy were left. Henry remembered that the other boy's dog had done all the right things.

The judge stepped to the center of the ring with a silver cup in his hand. Henry wasn't at all surprised when the judge handed it to the other boy. He just wondered why he hadn't been asked to leave the ring. He thought he must have made a mistake, but the judge said to Henry and the winner, "Come along to the main ring. There will be some more judging there."

Puzzled, Henry followed. Beezus and Ramona, Scooter, Mary Jane, and Robert, and their dogs followed Henry. Maybe Henry was going to win a prize after all.

In the main ring were the prize winners from all the other rings. Henry noticed two big silver

cups on the table and saw his judge whispering
to the other judges. They all looked at Ribsy.
Ribsy panted harder than ever. The judges had
the winners show their dogs again.

This time Henry wasn't taking any chances with the clothesline getting wound around his legs. He wound it around his hand so that there was only a foot of rope between his hand and Ribsy's collar. Ribsy did not behave any better the second time he was shown than he had the first. When Henry's turn came to lead him across the ring, he stopped to growl at a boxer. The boxer growled back.

Henry heard Scooter say, "If that mutt doesn't look out, he's going to get all bit up."

Ribsy growled louder. The snarling boxer advanced, dragging the little girl who owned him along on the end of his leash.

Henry tried to pull Ribsy away but Ribsy ignored him. The dogs circled around one another, pulling their owners after them. Henry yanked so hard at Ribsy's collar the dog choked. The boxer snarled and sprang at Ribsy, using his powerful front paws to knock over the smaller dog. Henry's hand was wound in the rope and he could not let go. He was pulled down on his stomach with his face in the grass.

"Look! Henry's in a dog fight!" screamed Beezus in great excitement.

The boxer's owner began to cry.

Henry was so mixed up he wasn't sure what was happening. He smelled the damp grass and felt it tickling his nose. He could hear snarls, growls, and barks. He could hear children scream-ing and yelling. The boxer stepped on his back. Henry said, "Oof!" He lifted his face from the grass in time to see a boy scout try to stop the fight by throwing a pan of water at the dogs. He missed the dogs but he didn't miss Henry.

Two judges ran into the ring and grabbed the dogs by their hind legs. They yanked the snarling animals apart.

"All right, son. Go ahead," ordered one judge, while the other helped the little girl hold her boxer.

Embarrassed and dripping, Henry got up from

the grass and, without looking either right or left, hurried Ribsy across the ring and back.

Finally only Henry and another boy were left. The judge stepped to the center of the ring. "The big cup for the best dog in the whole show goes to the boy with the setter." Everybody clapped when he handed the boy one of the big silver cups. Ribsy growled at the winner.

"And now," said the judge, "the cup for the most unusual dog in the show goes to the boy with the a—a—mixed-breed dog!" He handed Henry the other big silver cup.

"Gee, thanks," was all Henry could say. The audience clapped and he heard Beezus shout, "Hooray for Henry!" He thought Ribsy looked pleased.

Everyone gathered around to admire his cup until a newspaper photographer asked them to stand back while he took a picture of Henry and his dog and wrote down his name and address. Henry was going to have his picture in the paper!

"Congratulations," said Scooter, "but I still think he's a mutt."

"Well, anyway, he won a bigger cup than Rags," boasted Henry, "but I guess Rags is a pretty good dog, too. Good old Ribsy. Now we'll get you a drink of water."

He led Ribsy to the nearest drinking fountain. He filled the silver cup with water and put it on the ground. Ribsy greedily lapped the water. Henry patted him. "Good old Ribsy. I knew you wouldn't drink out of any dish but your own."

CHAPTER SIX

Finders
Keepers

AFTER lunch on the Saturday after the dog show Henry was in his room feeding his catfish. He dropped a tiny pinch of food into the water and watched it drift down to the bottom of the aquarium, where the catfish busily dug through the sand to find it.

"He-e-e-nry!" Robert was calling from the front yard.

Henry put the lid back on his aquarium and went out on the front porch. "Hi. What do you want?"

"Come on out and let's practice tumbling like the fellows in the gym at the Y."

"O.K." Henry ran down the front steps. Ribsy looked up from the bone he was gnawing and growled. It was not a cross growl. It was a growl that meant, "Don't bother me. Can't you see I'm busy?"

The boys practiced standing on their hands and turning somersaults on the lawn until Robert said, "Come on, let's try that trick where one fellow gets on his back with his feet in the air and the other fellow gets on top of his feet and the first fellow turns him around and around." He flopped on the grass with his feet in the air. "Come on. Try it," he said.

Henry sat on Robert's feet and lay back with his arms and legs outstretched. Robert tried to twirl him around. Henry teetered.

"Hey, you're kicking me!" Henry toppled over upon Robert.

"Oof!" Robert sat up. "You're too heavy. Let's try something else."

"I know what. Let's go over to Beezus' house

and practice chinning ourselves on her chestnut tree."

They found the girls in front of Beezus' house. They were busy tying a long jumping rope from the horse chestnut tree across the sidewalk to the lilac bush. Ramona, who was wearing pink coveralls and curlers in her hair, was scratching on the bark of the chestnut tree with her fingernails.

"Hi," said Henry.

"Hello," answered Beezus, stopping work on the rope.

"Mewow, mewow," said Ramona.

"What does she mean, 'Mewow'?" asked Henry.

"Oh, don't pay any attention to her," answered Beezus. "That's the way she says miaow. She's pretending she's a cat."

"Mewow," said Ramona and patted the curlers in her hair. "I'm a cat with curly hair."

Henry and Robert exchanged disgusted looks. Girls certainly started to be dumb when they were awfully young. They watched the girls in silence.

Then they all sat down on the grass and waited.

"I wish you'd go away," said Mary Jane at last. "We're busy."

"Don't mind us," said Henry. "We have all day."

Beezus tightened the knot on the jumping rope. "Henry Huggins! I think you're mean. Why don't you play in your own yard?"

"We want to watch what you're doing," answered Henry, chewing on a blade of grass.

"Ho! I know. I'll bet you think you're going to be tight-rope walkers!" scoffed Robert. "Why don't you tie the rope up high? It's only about two feet off the ground."

"Dumbbell!" said Beezus. "Every time we walk across it without falling off we'll move it up a foot. I'll bet even people in circuses don't start practicing at the top of the circus tent. And they have nets under them, too."

"Aw, you can't even walk it when it's two feet off the ground," scoffed Henry. "I'll bet you couldn't walk it if it were one inch off the ground."

"You be quiet, Henry Huggins!" ordered Mary Jane. "Why don't you and Robert mind your own business? Go on, Beezus. Let's not pay any attention to them. They just think they're smart."

Beezus opened her mother's umbrella and held it in her right hand. As she stepped up on the rope, Mary Jane took hold of her left hand to steady her. The lilac bush bent under her weight, the rope sagged, and Beezus was standing on the sidewalk with the rope under her feet.

Robert and Henry hooted with laughter. "You sure look silly standing there on that rope with that umbrella in your hand!"

"You keep quiet!" snapped Beezus. "Let's see you do it if you think you're so smart."

Henry laughed harder. "She can't even walk it when it's a trillionth of an inch off the sidewalk!"

Robert rolled on the grass. "Not even if it's a billionth of a trillionth of an inch off the sidewalk!"

Beezus waved the umbrella. "You get off my property!"

"You can't make us!" yelled Henry.

"If you don't go home, I'll never speak to you as long as I live!" Beezus was really angry.

"Or me either." Mary Jane glared at the boys. "See if we care!"

Just then Scooter rode down the street on his bicycle. "Look!" he yelled. "No hands!"

The others stopped squabbling to watch. As Scooter approached, he bent slowly backward while he continued to pedal. When his head had almost touched the fender over the back wheel, the bicycle began to wobble. The handle bars turned and the bicycle headed for the curb. Scooter tried to sit up. It was too late. He had lost

his balance. The bicycle bounced up the curb and tumbled Scooter sprawling upon the grass. The bicycle, stopped by the chestnut tree, toppled over on top of him.

Robert and Henry hooted as Scooter sheepishly untangled himself from his bicycle. He rubbed his shin but didn't say anything. The children knew the fall must have hurt, but Scooter wasn't going to admit it.

"Well, anyway, I did it once," he said, carefully feeling his right elbow to make sure it wasn't broken.

"Aw, I'll bet you didn't." Henry was pleased. Usually he was the one to have accidents while Scooter watched.

"I did, too!"

"I bet you didn't."

"Keep quiet, all of you!" shouted Beezus. "And get off my property this minute!"

"Beezus, you keep out of this!" ordered Henry.

"Aw, you're just a dumb girl," sneered Scooter.

"Yes, a dumb girl," echoed Robert. "And anyway, it isn't your property."

"My dad pays rent on it, so it's just the same as my property." Beezus raised the umbrella to hit Scooter.

"Hit him!" yelled Mary Jane, far from her usual ladylike self.

"Don't you dare hit me!"

"Hey, you kids!"

It was a strange voice. The children stopped quarreling to see who it was. A strange boy was sitting astride a bicycle by the curb. He was a big boy, big enough to be in the seventh or eighth grade. He didn't belong on Klickitat Street and none of them had ever seen him before.

"I've been yelling at you for five minutes," he said and grinned. "Is one of you Henry Huggins?"

Henry was so surprised he didn't answer. Who was this boy and how did he know his name? Robert nudged Henry, who remembered he hadn't answered. "Oh yes," he said, "that's me."

The boy reached into the pocket of his jeans and pulled out the newspaper clipping that showed Henry and Ribsy at the dog show. Henry couldn't understand why this strange boy was carrying that picture with him. Just then Ribsy began to bark furiously and Henry saw him running down the street toward them.

"Dizzy!" the boy shouted and sprang from his bicycle. "Here, Dizzy!" Ribsy jumped up on the boy and licked his hands. The boy laughed and patted him and, when Ribsy would stand still long enough, scratched him behind his left ear.

That's funny, thought Henry. How does he know Ribsy likes to be scratched behind his left ear? And why does he call him Dizzy? "His name isn't Dizzy," he said to the boy. "It's Ribsy and he's my dog!"

Ribsy looked at the boy and wagged his tail again.

A terrible thought came to Henry. Ribsy must have belonged to the boy before he found him in the drugstore over a year ago. The boy had seen his picture in the paper and had come to take him away!

If only Ribsy hadn't won the prize in the dog show and had his picture in the paper! Then the boy would never have found him. Henry didn't know what to do. He couldn't give up Ribsy after a whole year. He couldn't.

He moved closer to Ribsy and put his hand on his collar. "He's my dog," he said. "He's my dog and you can't take him away. He was a skinny old dog when I found him and I bought him a collar and a license and a dish and now I buy him two pounds of horse meat every week and Woofies Dog Food besides. And I wash him and brush him and everything." Henry gulped. "You can't take him away!"

"Henry does take awfully good care of him," added Beezus loyally.

"Henry found him, so he must have run away from you," said Robert.

"Finders keepers, losers weepers," chanted Mary Jane.

"Well, I had him longer than you have," said the boy. "And I fed him and brushed him, too. I had him when he was a puppy. He used to chase his tail so much I named him Dizzy. And the only reason he ran away was because he was heart-broken. I went to Scout Camp for the summer and Mom and Dad went East and we left Dizzy with my aunt and uncle. They said he was so lonesome and homesick he wouldn't eat or play or anything. Then one day they couldn't find him anywhere. They thought maybe he'd gone home to look for me so they drove over to our house to look for him. He wasn't there and they looked every place. They advertised in the paper and everything."

"So he did run away," said Robert. "You left him and he ran away."

Ribsy licked the boy's hand again.

"Look. He remembers me and wants to come home with me."

"But he likes me, too," protested Henry.

Ribsy looked at Henry and wagged his tail.

For the first time Scooter spoke. "We like Ribsy right here in this neighborhood. He's just about the most popular dog around here and every one of us would miss him."

Henry stared at Scooter in amazement. It was the first time he had heard him say anything good about Ribsy.

"Yes, we all like him," agreed Robert. "All the kids at Glenwood School like him. He waits for Henry every day under the fir tree and all the kids know him."

"Yes, what about us?" asked Beezus. "Henry has taken care of him for a whole year and I don't think it's fair for you to take him away."

"He didn't have a collar or a license tag when I found him," said Henry.

"He had them when I went off to Scout Camp. I don't know how he lost them except my aunt said he was awfully thin when he disappeared. Maybe he slipped his collar off over his head or somebody took it." The boy reached in his pocket. "I have my birthday money that you can take." He held out a five-dollar bill to Henry.

"Five dollars! I wouldn't sell Ribsy for a million dollars!"

"Oh, I didn't mean for you to sell him," said the boy hastily. "I meant the money to help pay his expenses for the last year. I know it isn't enough, but it's all I have."

Henry felt sorry for the boy. He could understand why he would want to keep a smart dog like Ribsy. But Henry couldn't part with his dog. Nothing exciting had ever happened to him before and look at all the things that had happened this year!

Henry knelt and put his arm around his dog's neck. "You wouldn't want to leave me, would you, Ribsy? You wouldn't want to leave Klickitat Street, would you?"

Ribsy licked Henry's face.

The stranger knelt and snapped his fingers.

"Dizzy, you want to come home with me, don't you?"

Ribsy looked at him, wagged his tail, and said, "Woof!"

"I guess he likes both of us," sighed Henry. "But I don't care. He ran away from you and I found him."

"That's right. Just like I said, Finders keepers, losers weepers," said Mary Jane.

"But I raised him from a pup. And my mother and father and kid sister miss him, too."

"But he likes to meet me after school and play with the kids." Henry paused to pet the dog. Then he said slowly, "Maybe we should let Ribsy decide."

"Sure," said Scooter. "That's a good idea. Don't worry, Henry. He'll choose you."

"That seems fair enough," agreed the boy. "How shall we let him choose?"

"I know," said Scooter. "Leave Ribsy where he is and each of you go twenty squares down the sidewalk in opposite directions. Then when I say, 'Go!' you both start calling at the same time. Whichever one Ribsy goes to gets to keep the dog."

"O.K.," agreed Henry. He felt all quivery inside.

"Sounds fair to me," agreed the boy.

"Oh, Henry, what if he doesn't choose you?" asked Beezus fearfully.

"Don't worry," said Mary Jane. "He won't want to leave Henry."

Scooter held Ribsy by his collar. Henry counted twenty squares down the sidewalk toward his house. The boy walked twenty the other way. They both turned and faced the dog. Henry's mouth felt so dry he was afraid he might not be able to call.

Scooter turned to the boy. "Say, you don't have any meat or anything in your pockets, do you?" he asked suspiciously.

"No, I don't. Cross my heart."

"How about you, Henry?" Scooter was going to be fair.

Henry gulped. "No, me neither."

"O.K. We want to make this a fair contest."

"Good luck, Henry!" shouted Beezus.

"Thanks," said Henry weakly.

Scooter turned Ribsy toward the street so he was facing neither Henry nor the strange boy. "All right, you guys. Ready, get set—go!" He took his hand off Ribsy's collar.

"Here, Ribsy! Here, Ribsy! Come on, Ribs!" At least Henry's voice worked.

"Here, Dizzy, Dizzy, Dizzy!"

The dog's former master snapped his fingers.

The dog looked at Henry. He looked at the other boy. Then he sat down to scratch behind his left ear with his left hind foot.

"Ribsy!" wailed Henry. "Come here! Here, Ribsy! Here, Ribsy!"

"Come, Dizzy! Come, Dizzy!" called the boy.

Ribsy stood up and took a few steps toward the boy and wagged his tail. The children groaned.

"Ribsy!" shouted Henry with a sinking feeling in his stomach. Ribsy stopped, turned around, wagged his tail, and said, "Woof!"

"Attaboy, Ribsy!" shouted Henry.

"Go on, Ribsy!" screamed Beezus.

"No coaching from the audience!" ordered Scooter.

Ribsy took a few steps toward Henry. Then he looked back at the other boy.

"Horse meat, Ribsy, horse meat! Here, Ribsy! Here, Ribsy!" At the mention of horse meat Ribsy looked at Henry.

"Here, Dizzy, Dizzy!" Then the boy had an idea. "Here, Ribsy! Here, Ribsy!" he called.

"Hey, you're cheating!" objected Henry. "I'm supposed to call him Ribsy."

"There wasn't any rule about what we should call him."

"That's right, Henry," agreed Scooter.

"Look, he's turning around!" shouted Mary Jane.

But Ribsy only turned around to chew at a spot near his tail. He bit at the flea, sat down, scratched behind his left ear again, and then stood up. The boys kept on yelling.

With a tired sigh Ribsy sank down on the sidewalk, put his head on his paws, and closed his eyes.

The children groaned. "Don't go to sleep now, Ribsy!" begged Henry, who was so scared his hands felt cold and damp.

Ribsy opened his eyes and, without moving his head, turned them first toward the strange boy and then toward Henry. "Come on, Ribsy," they both coaxed.

Slowly Ribsy stood up, and after a backward glance at the stranger, trotted eight squares down the sidewalk toward Henry. He paused, scratched again, and trotted the remaining squares to Henry. Then he sank down with his head on Henry's foot and closed his eyes again.

Ribsy had chosen Henry!

The children cheered, but Henry couldn't say a word. He knelt and hugged his dog.

"I knew he'd choose you, Henry," crowed Mary Jane. "I just knew it all the time."

"My, but I was scared for a minute," said Beezus.

The other boy looked so disappointed that Henry couldn't help feeling sorry for him. "I'm glad Ribsy wants to stay with me," said Henry, "but I'm sorry you have to lose him. He's an awfully good dog."

"I hate to lose him, too, but I guess I can't complain. It was a fair contest." The boy threw his leg over his bicycle. "Say, do you suppose I could come over to see him sometimes?"

"Sure. Any time you want."

"Thanks. I'll be around soon." The boy rode off down the street.

The children all crowded around Ribsy to pet him. "I sure am lucky," said Henry, "but he had me scared for a while."

"Jeepers, I don't know what this neighborhood would have done without Ribsy," said Beezus. "Come on. Now that Ribsy is Henry's for keeps, let's think of something we all can play."